# DESPERATE DOMINATION

EVERLY STONE

# DESPERATE DOMINATION

*Bought by the Billionaire*
*Book Three*

By Everly Stone

Created with Vellum

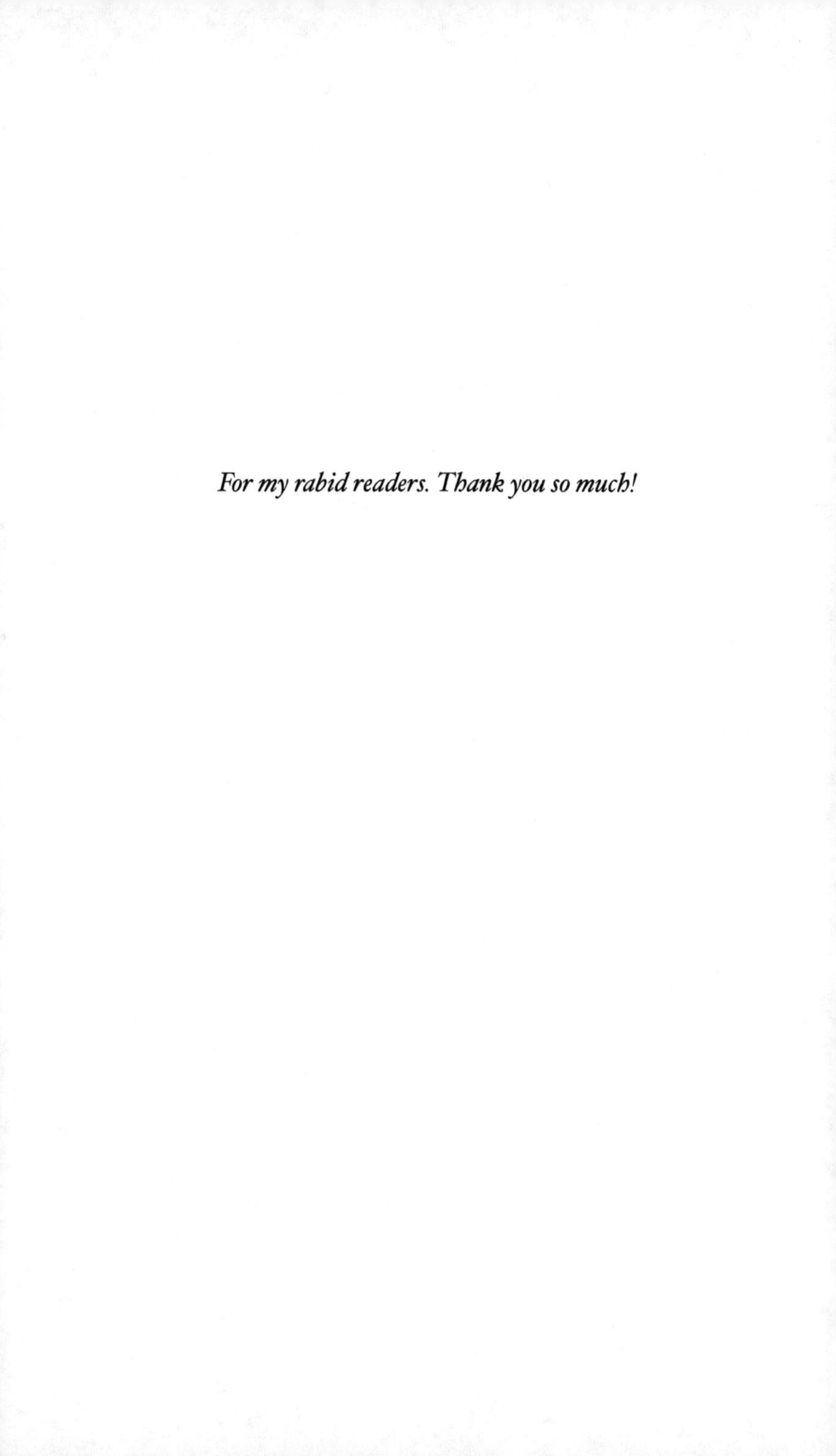

*For my rabid readers. Thank you so much!*

## ALSO BY EVERLY STONE

Learn more at Everly's website

https://www.everlystone.com.

**Bought by the Billionaire**

**The Series**

(HOT novellas, must be read in order)

*Dark Domination*

*Deep Domination*

*Desperate Domination*

*Divine Domination*

**Kidnapped by the Billionaire**

**The Series**

(HOT novellas, must be read in order)

*Filthy Wicked Love*

*Crazy Beautiful Love*

*One More Shameless Night*

**Under His Command**

**The Series**

(HOT novellas, must be read in order)

*Controlling her Pleasure*

*Commanding her Trust*

*Claiming her Heart*

## The Snowed in Series

*Snowbound with the Billionaire*

*Snowed in with the Boss*

# ABOUT THE BOOK

**WARNING: This is a white-hot, panty-melting, boundary-pushing read. Not intended for the faint of heart.**

*"You're mine. You belong to me. You will always belong to me. Because no one has ever made you feel the way I have."*

Jackson Hawke might be a monster, but he's Hannah's monster. They belong together and she's determined to show Jackson she can love every part of him-light and dark, cruel and gentle, lost soul and Dominant man.

Jackson knows he doesn't deserve her. He is broken and twisted and wrong inside, but when Hannah touches him it feels right, *he* feels right in a way he hasn't in so long.

Can a monster learn to become a man again? Or will dark forces from the past claim Hannah's life before she can claim his heart?

* * Desperate Domination is the 3rd in the Bought by the Billionaire serial romance series and ends in a CLIFFHANGER. For maximum enjoyment it should be read after books one and two. Same steamy romance, new author name.* *

# CHAPTER ONE

## Harley

*Six Years Ago*

Before you embark on a journey of revenge, you should dig two graves.

Or so Confucius said.

Harley Mason had never been the type to put stock in conventional wisdom. She resented authority figures—even those who had died thousands of years ago—and didn't believe anyone in the unjust, uncaring, fucked up world had answers to the big questions. People were crazy and the ones who considered themselves sufficiently enlightened to dispense wisdom to the masses were usually the craziest of all.

She preferred to trust in her gut, her wits, and the sharp-toothed creature deep inside of her that demanded debts be paid. She'd learned at a young age that life wasn't fair, but she refused to believe it had to stay that way. The cheaters could be caught, the untouchables brought low, and the wicked crushed beneath the boot of her uniquely heartless brand of justice.

The man who had destroyed her mother deserved to suffer.

Not long before Harley's ninth birthday, Emma Mason had disappeared, leaving nothing behind but a note saying, "The heart wants what it wants." Harley and her twin sister, Hannah, had suffered through the usual stages of grief after a traumatic loss and resigned themselves to living without a mother when, early one morning nearly a year after Emma had vanished, she'd reappeared at the front gate, a half-starved, anxiety-riddled shadow of the woman she'd been. Their mother's body had come home, but her spirit had never returned.

Before, Emma had helped with homework after school and sent the staff home early so she and her daughters could make dinner together, choosing recipes from her favorite French cookbook. After, she abandoned Harley and Hannah to the care of their nannies during the school year and their Aunt Sybil during the summers. She acted as if it pained her to set eyes on her children, but Emma was too relentlessly miserable for Harley to take it personally. Her mother also shunned walks in the garden, good books, charity work, her sewing room, afternoons in the kitchen making coq au vin, and almost everything else that had once given her joy.

No, Harley didn't blame her mother for being broken. She blamed the person who had broken her. She swore to herself that someday she would make the man pay, and finally, after years of searching for clues to the stranger's identity, she'd learned his name.

Ian Hawke.

And so she had launched her summer of revenge—intending to shatter Ian's son and teach the bastard what if felt like to see someone you love ruined forever—and she hadn't regretted a moment of it.

Until now.

Now, as the car rolled down the side of the mountain, each horrifying revolution seeming to last forever as Harley realized she was about to die, she wished she could take it all back. She wished she could go back to the beginning of the summer and spend it in Paris instead of on the Virginia shore. She wished she'd never met Jackson Hawke or tricked him into loving her. She wished she'd never filed the false report with the military police or doctored evidence to make sure Jackson would be found guilty of a crime he hadn't committed.

But most of all, she wished she'd never seduced Jackson's best friend. She wished she'd never met Clay, never loved him, and never agreed to run away and get married this weekend. If she could take it all back, she would, and then Clay wouldn't be dying in this car beside her.

*Should have dug three graves.*

Three graves. One for her, one for Jackson, her enemy's son, and one for Clay, the only man Harley had ever loved.

"I love you. I'm so sorry," she sobbed, reaching for Clay's arm as the car's roof bounced off the ground and they spun upright once more. But the sound of metal screaming, as it caved in around them, made it impossible to hear her own voice.

Later, when she came to, hanging upside down by her seatbelt with Clay dangling beside her, his eyes wide and death stiffening his handsome face, she would regret that most of all. He hadn't heard her say that she loved him one last time, and he didn't know that she was sorry.

"I'm so sorry," she sobbed, tears streaming up her forehead to run into her hair, stinging into a cut on her scalp. "It should have been me. I wish it were me, Clay. I'm so sorry."

She cupped his face in one shaking hand, leaving a mark behind on his cool cheek. In the moonlight streaming in through the crumpled windows, the blood smear looked black. Harley stared at it, strangely mesmerized by the thickness of it and the slow drip, drip, drip as the cut on her arm leaked onto the roof below her.

She was still hanging there, tears flowing the wrong way and her pulse slowing to a dangerous—*thud...du-dud....dud*—when a hand punched through the web of crinkled glass on the passenger side, making her flinch and cry out.

"It's Dominic," came a low, lightly accented voice. "Are you hurt?"

"Clay's dead," she whimpered, not turning to look at the dark-eyed boy her father had hired to follow her around this summer.

Dominic was allegedly part of a security team hired to protect her—her father said he'd been receiving threats from an old business rival—but Harley suspected Daddy was simply using that as an excuse to spy on her. She'd come by her sneaky streak honestly and had learned not to trust her father around the same time she'd learned to walk.

Any other summer, she would have had an affair with Dominic, just to piss off dear old Dad—he hated it when she fucked the help—but she'd been too busy ruining two men's lives to have time for the slim Puerto Rican boy with the kind eyes.

"I'm sorry," Dom said as he reached for her seatbelt. "Let me help you out."

"Stop." She shoved at his hand as it fumbled near her waist. "Go away. I won't leave him."

"We have to go, Harley," Dom insisted. "This wasn't an accident. I saw the truck that pushed you off the road. It was the same one that's been parked outside the bar for the past two weeks."

"What?" Harley's question became a moan as Dom succeeded in releasing the seatbelt. She slumped down onto the dented roof, every bruise on her body crying out in protest.

"It was the man in the camo hat," he said, helping her shift onto her back. "The one who was watching you at the bar. He was at your apartment complex tonight and followed you when you left. I tried to call your cell to warn you, but there was no answer."

"I had the ringer off," she said, lips moving numbly. She'd always turned her ringer off when she was with Clay, just in case Jackson called. She hadn't wanted to explain why she was still taking phone calls from a man she claimed frightened her.

When she'd told Clay that Jackson had hit her, he'd been devastated, his usually smiling blue eyes filling with so much pain that, for a moment, she had wished she could reel the lie back between her lips. But back then, hurting Jackson's father had mattered more than sparing the best man she'd ever met. Back then, she'd been too stupid to realize that she'd finally found a love bigger than all the bitterness and hate.

If only she'd laid down her weapons and walked away before it was too late.

"We need to get you somewhere safe,"

Dom said with a sigh. "If this guy is a professional, he'll want to make sure you're dead before he reports back to whoever he's working for."

Dom pulled her through the window, dragging her spine against the twisted metal of the crumpled frame. Every inch of her body throbbed with distress, the wounds she'd inflicted to fake her police report providing a dull background agony to the wail of new injuries. She'd lost a lot of blood and when Dom helped her to her feet, the world spun in great looping circles.

"Lean into me." He grunted, tightening the arm banded around her waist. "I need you to stay awake, Harley."

"I'm awake," she mumbled as she staggered along beside him, following a narrow trail through the woods.

She was awake and alive and Clay was dead.

Clay was dead.

Clay was *dead.*

The horrible mantra thrummed through her thoughts, drawing a sob from deep in her chest. She didn't want to get to safety; she wanted to lie down next to Clay and wait for someone to send her to the other side to find him.

She'd never believed in heaven or hell, but the way she loved Clay made her hope this wasn't the end. It couldn't be, not when they were just getting started, when she'd finally realized that there was something more important than revenge. There was love, blue eyes filled with laughter, and a man whose kiss softened the once impenetrable walls around her heart.

But now those lips were cold and she would never kiss them again.

Her knees buckled as she went limp with grief, sliding down the side of Dom's wiry body.

"Stand up," he ordered, hitching her higher. "I can't carry you up the side of the mountain, Harley. I need you to walk."

"I can't." She sobbed, her head bowing over her chest. Clay could have carried her. Jackson too. She'd had two brave, strong men devoted to her and she'd destroyed them both. Clay was dead and Jackson would wish he were dead—sooner or later—and it was all her fault.

She was poison, just like her father, just like Ian Hawke. She was a predator who had taken pleasure in other people's pain and now she would pay for it a thousand times over. She would never know peace or an end to the crushing guilt of knowing she had killed the man she loved.

"If you don't start walking, they're going to find us," Dom whispered, his fingers digging painfully into the bruised flesh at her hip. "And then we'll both be as dead as your boyfriend."

He was right. Someone was coming. The hairs at the back of her neck stood on end, warning that the hunter had become the hunted.

Swallowing hard, Harley forced strength back into her knees and began to put one foot in front of the other. She didn't care if she were murdered, but Dominic didn't deserve to die this way. He was only trying to do his job and if she'd answered his call, Clay might be alive.

Dom wasn't to blame. She was in this mess because of her stubborn insistence that those who'd wronged her should pay for their sins a thousand times over.

A thousand times a thousand times a thousand.

In the years that followed, as fate ensured there was no way to forget the horrible things she'd done, Harley paid the price for that one terrible summer again and again. Every morning she woke with the reminder that Clay had died too soon staring her in the face, and every night she went to bed wondering if she would ever stop aching for the man she'd destroyed.

And then, one night the past caught up with her, and she learned that no matter how high a price you've paid, there is always something left to lose.

# CHAPTER TWO

## Hannah

*Present Day*

F*aster, Hannah! Run faster. Faster!*

Hitching the red chiffon of her dress up around her knees, Hannah sprinted as fast as she could down the road toward what she hoped was civilization.

But her legs still ached from the six-mile hike earlier and she'd only choked down a few bites of food.

She was exhausted, running on empty, and there was no way she would make it to safety before Jackson tracked her down. The jungle on the left side of the road was too thick for her to penetrate and the shoreline to the right offered little to no cover. If she stayed on the road, it wasn't a matter of *if* Jackson would find her, but when.

Unless she found a way to escape that he wouldn't suspect...

With a quick glance over her shoulder to make sure no tall, terrifying men had appeared on the road, Hannah darted off the gravel and across the dunes toward the beach.

The sand ended a few feet from the ocean, replaced by a line of jagged black rocks that seemed to grimace at the sea, daring it to take its best shot. The tide was low, but fierce, slamming into the stones with a ferocity that made her shiver.

If she didn't jump far enough or swim hard enough, she would be tossed back toward the shore and dashed to pieces on the rocks long before Jackson or anyone else could find her. She was a strong swimmer, but she didn't know this stretch of shoreline.

She didn't know the tide patterns or the reef nearby or what kind of ocean life claimed this part of the island as their territory.

Back home, she knew which beaches were her best bet for observing giant sea turtles, which were good for snorkeling or boogie boarding, and which to avoid because of dangerous rip tides.

Or sharks.

There was a bay to the far north of the island where shark attacks were quadruple the number of anywhere else in the region. It was their feeding ground and anyone with sense knew to stay out of the water. Even the tourists knew, their guidebooks containing strongly worded warnings about the likelihood of shark attack and grisly stories of the people who had lost their lives in the bay over the years.

Looking out at the churning water, where sea foam frothed pink in the setting sun, Hannah couldn't see anything beneath the water except occasional dark patches indicating coral formations.

But that didn't mean there was nothing to see and dusk was a dangerous time to swim. Sharks hunted from dusk until dawn and as soon as she hit the water, she would be prey.

*You're already prey, fool.*

Hannah swallowed hard.

Her inner voice was right.

She was Jackson's prey and she had no idea what he would do to her if he caught her. He might lock her in that cage she'd seen Adam carrying to the back of the house or something worse.

And at least with a shark she knew how to fight back.

Sharks preferred easy prey. If you managed to get a few solid punches in to their nose and eyes, most would swim away looking for a less feisty food source. Jackson, on the other hand, would take pleasure from overpowering her while she struggled, showing her who controlled her, body and soul.

"No," she said aloud, her hands fisting at her sides.

She was in control now and she had to stay that way.

No matter how much a part of her wanted to believe that she could trust Jackson, she couldn't gamble her life on it. She'd made the choice to run and now she had to see it through.

Without letting herself think too much about the things lurking beneath the water or the vicious crash of the waves as they pounded against the shore, Hannah toed off her sandals and unzipped her dress. The fabric fell to her feet, leaving her in nothing but her strapless bra and panties. It wasn't a swimsuit, but it would leave her body at least partially covered so that she wouldn't have to approach a potential rescuer buck-naked.

The cool ocean breeze whispered across her skin, raising gooseflesh on her arms and legs as she picked her way across the dark rocks, getting as far from the shore as she could without being sucked into the waves.

As she reached the outer most point, just before the rocks dropped away into deeper water, she exhaled long and slow, her fingers wiggling at her sides as she waited for the perfect moment.

As soon as the next wave crashed against the shore and began its rush away, she jumped, leaping into the churning froth.

The ocean closed around her, cool and shocking, but she didn't waste time allowing her body to adjust to the water temperature before bobbing back to the surface and pulling hard toward the open sea.

She made it a good ten feet out before the next wave bore down hard upon her, trying to toss her back the way she'd come. Diving beneath the curl, she slipped beyond the reach of the strongest onshore current and turned left, swimming parallel to the shore.

Thankfully, the current seemed to be on her side, drawing her south toward the other end of the island.

Ignoring her racing heart, Hannah established a rhythm with her strokes and did her best to keep her breath under control. She was used to swimming a mile or more every morning before bustling around the bed and breakfast cleaning and taking care of guests.

If she kept calm and used her body efficiently, she could easily swim five miles or more and hopefully come across some sign of life along the shore.

The island was small, but surely there had to be some indigenous population.

She would look for boat docks or cleared beaches and be ready to head back in toward land when she spotted them. She would find help and she would get off this island in one piece. She had to stay positive and focused or fear would swallow her whole.

Over the past week, she had convinced herself that Jackson wasn't as frightening or cruel as she'd thought at first. She'd convinced herself that he cared and that she wasn't in any serious danger. But the moment she'd started down the road away from the house where she'd been held captive, those pretty lies had vanished in a wave of terror.

Now, when she imagined Jackson finding her, it wasn't the man who had touched a soft finger to her lips that she saw in her mind's eye. It was the man who had balled his hands into fists when she'd smiled at him, the one who had promised to break her and looked like he would enjoy doing it.

*Just keep swimming,* she thought, trying to talk her heart down from her throat. *Just keep swimming.*

She sounded like that fish from the Disney movie, the one she'd gone to see when she was in high school even though Harley had said they were too old for cartoons.

But even back then, when she was fifteen and discovering boys while learning to drive, Hannah had known she would never be too old for cartoons. She would never be too old for anything that brought her joy.

There was no reason to outgrow simple pleasures.

There was no reason to shut out the things that made her happy because she was growing up.

She didn't have to be like her parents.

There was too much magic in the world to become bitter and jaded and growing up didn't have to mean growing old. She had always believed that and secretly thought that holding on to childlike wonder would make her a better mother, the kind who understood what her children were going through because she'd never let go of the child inside of herself.

But after a week under Jackson's control, a good deal of it spent in isolation with nothing to occupy her thoughts or distract her from taking a hard look at the state of her life, she realized she would never be a mom. She would never have a husband or children because she was going to spend the rest of her life addicted to the touch of a man who didn't care if she lived or died.

Jackson didn't love her—he didn't even know her true identity—but she would crave his touch until the day they put her in the ground. He'd summoned a darkly sensual part of her to the surface and there would be no putting it back to sleep.

She would always long for his firm hand and the erotic bliss of being under his control.

She might escape him today, but he would haunt her forever, no matter how far or how fast she ran.

Her thoughts were depressing to say the least, but that wasn't why she sank lower in the water, her head dipping below the surface before she bobbed back above the waves. It was the pain that made her falter, a sharp agony knotting low in her legs.

Hannah winced, crying out as another wave of suffering flashed through her calf muscles. The cramps were so intense they soon rendered her numb from the knees down. Fighting the urge to panic, she strained harder with her arms, trying to compensate for her suddenly useless legs.

All she wanted to do was stop swimming and dig her thumbs into her aching calves, but if she stopped pulling with her arms, she would drown.

While she struggled, willing her thrumming muscles to relax, a larger wave swept in, taking her by surprise. She sucked in a breath at the wrong time, taking in a mouthful of seawater as she was rolled beneath the curl.

She broke the surface again in the trough, coughing up ocean, fighting to catch her breath before the next wave hit, but she barely had time to clear her lungs before she was swept under again.

Chest aching with the need for oxygen, Hannah tumbled through the dark, the muffled thunder of the churning water above her roaring in her ears. As she revolved, she became aware of a sucking sensation tugging at her torso, drawing her farther from the shore, out into the wilds of the open sea.

In some still, quiet hall inside her mind, a

sober voice announced that she was caught in a rip current and would likely die before she made it back to shore. If she had the use of her legs, she might be able to fight her way free by swimming parallel to the beach until the current let her go, but without her legs this was most likely a lost cause.

Chances were that she was about to drown.

Her body would be lost to the ocean and her Aunt Sybil left alone in the world, with no idea what had happened to her niece.

Jackson wouldn't know what had become of her either.

The thought shouldn't hurt, but it did. She'd run from him tonight, but deep down she'd expected to see him again, somewhere, someday. She'd never imagined it would end this way, with her dead and him forever haunted by his unanswered questions.

The thought made her soul howl with regret.

She didn't want to go out like this. She didn't want to lose her life in the middle of running from her problems, the way she always had.

She was tired of running, tired of being afraid. She wanted to face her fears—to face Jackson—and come away a better person for proving that she was stronger than anyone gave her credit for.

She might be submissive, but she wasn't subhuman.

She didn't deserve Jackson's contempt or abuse. She should have stayed, told him the truth, and insisted he believe her. She should have stood up to him and shown that she could be every bit as persistent and stubborn as the man she was falling in love with.

He inspired so many conflicting feelings, but love was there, threading through the fear, a ray of light in the darkness.

But if she didn't get back to shore, he would never know that one of the Mason twins had truly cared for him and wanted nothing more than to give him pleasure and ease his pain.

Drawing strength from her thoughts, Hannah pulled hard to the surface, managing to get in three long strokes before another wave bore down on her, forcing her beneath the water. She dove down, ears ringing and legs stinging with soreness, but she refused to let terror take over.

As soon as she was able, she resurfaced and flipped over onto her back to float. If she could draw in a few easier breaths and get her racing pulse under control, she would have the strength to keep fighting.

She was in the midst of her second smooth inhalation—and silently congratulating herself on keeping her head in the midst of a crisis—

when an arm wrapped around her chest, banding beneath her armpits.

Surprised, she flinched, but the arm only tightened its inexorable grip around her ribs.

A moment later, Jackson's ragged breath warmed her ear. "Lie still and let me help you. Fight me and I'll drag you back to shore unconscious."

With a shudder of relief, Hannah relaxed into him, going limp to make her body easier to tow out of the rip tide.

Clearly sensing her surrender, Jackson kicked hard beneath the water, his powerful legs sending them gliding toward the beach on the crest of the next wave. She could feel the current tugging at her thighs, but it was still hard to believe that Jackson was fighting the full force of the ocean to get them both to safety.

He was, as ever, in control of himself and all he surveyed.

The immense strength and power of the man hit home long before they reached the shallow water and he pulled her into his arms, carrying her out of the waves like she weighed nothing at all.

But it was the moment he laid her down in the sand—gently, carefully—that impressed her the most.

Any man could bulk up until he was the biggest beast in the jungle, not any man could communicate with a touch that he believed the world was a better place with you in it.

"You almost died," he growled as he swiped water from his face, his voice a low rumble that threatened an impending storm. "If I hadn't seen your dress blow into the road, you would be dead right now."

Hannah stared up at him, still breathing hard. "Maybe not. I was fighting. I might have made it."

Heat flashed through his eyes as he braced his hands on either side of her shoulders. "Or you might be dead. You might be at the bottom of the ocean because lying to me is more important to you than your damned life!"

"Lies are the only things you'll believe," she shot back, refusing to be cowed by his anger. "You wouldn't recognize the truth if it walked up and slapped you in the face, Jackson Hawke."

"You don't have permission to—"

"I will call you what I want, when I want," she barreled on, tears rising in her eyes. "I don't want to be your property; I want to be your friend. Because I c-care about you. Even if you are mean and dangerous and probably out of your damned mind."

"You care about me," he echoed, his expression going blank in that way he had, the way that made her unsure whether she was going to earn pleasure or pain from his hands.

But right now she was too fresh from near-death to be afraid of the consequences of her frank speech.

"Yes, I care about you." She blinked faster, trying to keep her tears from slipping down her cheeks "But I'm probably as crazy as you are you big, stupid, arrogant—"

Jackson's lips found hers, silencing her with a kiss. His tongue slipped into her mouth, mating with hers, sending electricity searing across her chilled skin and a roar of approval thundering through her every cell.

She relaxed her jaw, welcoming his invasion with a moan as she wrapped her arms around his neck.

She clung to him, each press of her fingertips into his muscled shoulders a promise that she would never let him go. He might be mean and dangerous and crazy, but he cared about her, too.

She could feel it in the way he pulled her close, rolling her on top of him as he claimed her with his kiss.

# CHAPTER THREE

## Jackson

He didn't know up from down or right from wrong. All he knew was that he needed her. He needed to be inside of her, to prove to both of them that she was still alive.

Thank God she was still alive. If he'd lost her...

If he'd been forced to watch her die...

He couldn't think about it. He wouldn't think about that or anything else.

Driving a hand into her wet hair, he fisted the other in her panties, ripping them away with one swift jerk. She cried out against his lips as the satin tore, but when he tugged at the back of her thigh, guiding it to the outside of his hip, she spread her legs without resistance. He smoothed his palm over her ass, tracing the seam of her buttock until he dipped his fingers between her legs, finding where she was already slick and hot.

"No more lies," he said, shoving two digits deep into her pussy, summoning another moan from low in her throat. "From now on, you tell me the truth or I will show you how mean and crazy I can be. Do you hear me?"

"You don't scare me," she said, nipping his bottom lip between her teeth hard enough to send pain coursing through his jaw.

"You don't scare me, sir," he corrected as he delivered a stern swat to her bare ass, falling back into the game.

He understood the game. The game had rules and a logic that was easy to follow. He didn't know what to do with this woman when she refused to play by the rules, when she told him she cared about him in that sweet, sad voice that made his heart want to believe her, even if his mind knew better.

"Yes, sir," she said, easing the tension in his chest. "You don't scare me, sir."

"I should." He released the close of her bra and tossed it away. Her breasts fell heavily onto his chest, making his cock throb. He cupped her fullness in his hands, pinching her nipples until she cried out and her hips began to squirm, restlessly seeking the friction of his erection between her legs.

"Because I don't love you," he continued in his hardest voice. "I told you, the man who cared about you is dead. Even if I wanted to, I could never love you, or anyone else, ever again."

"I thought you said no more lies," she said, arching her back, pressing her breasts more firmly into his palms.

"I'm not lying." He kneed her legs apart and bowed upward, lifting her into the air as he pressed his cock against her through the drenched fabric of his boxer briefs. "I don't love you, and I don't want to make love to you. I want to fuck you until you scream and realize what a stupid decision it was to run from me."

"Then fuck me until I scream, sir," she said, a flush spreading from her breasts up her throat to her gently parted lips. "Fuck me until I know who I belong to."

God *damn.*

He didn't want to give her the upper hand, even for a second, but there was no way he could resist an invitation like that.

Clenching his jaw tight, he reversed their positions, rolling her beneath him as he shoved his soaked boxers down his thighs. He kicked the fabric free and reached down, spreading her outer lips with his thumbs, revealing the slick, swollen flesh of her pussy.

*His* pussy. She was his and he was going to make sure that every time she sat down for the next three days she remembered it.

He positioned the dripping head of his cock and shoved home with a brutal thrust that wrenched the promised scream from her lips. The sound was part pleasure, part pain, and so fucking sexy he couldn't have held back if he'd tried.

With a groan of surrender, he braced his arms on either side of her pretty face and rode her hard. He fucked her until her breasts bounced against his chest and the sound of their bodies connecting made a dull thudding sound audible over the crash of the waves against the shore. They were both going to be sore as hell tomorrow, but he didn't care. He needed her to feel him, every inch of his cock filling her up, staking his claim.

Her pleasure and pain belonged to him. *She* belonged to him.

"You're mine," he said, biting his bottom lip as he fought for control, for the strength to hold on until he felt her go. "You belong to me. Even if you kill yourself, even if you kill me, you will always belong to me."

"Oh God, Jackson, please!" Her nails raked down his arms, leaving stinging trails behind that he knew would fill with blood.

But he didn't care. Let her mark him. Let her bleed him, so long as she came begging him for more.

"Please what?" He shifted the angle of his thrusts until her breath caught on a gasp of pleasure.

"Can I come?" she asked, voice rising as she writhed beneath him, fighting to hold back the wave mounting inside of her. "Please, sir, can I come? Please? God, Jackson, please!"

"Come," he commanded, shoving into her one final time. She cried out his name and he roared something incomprehensible into the soft curve of her neck as her pussy clenched tight around his cock, triggering an orgasm so intense he lost time.

For a moment, he existed outside of reality, in an alternate dimension where there was nothing but warmth and pleasure and the smell of this woman all around him. And it was sweet, so sweet he thought maybe he could die a happy man as long as he died with the smell of her thick in his head, the taste of her on his tongue, the feel of her arms and legs locked around him, holding him close to her heart.

He came and came, pleasure having its way with him for what could have been hours before he finally collapsed on top of her, fighting to regain his breath. Between the battle with the ocean and the erotic battle with his newly recaptured prisoner, he was too spent to move, even when he realized that he hadn't pulled out. He'd come inside her, spilling every drop into the slick heat of her pussy.

He cursed himself but didn't roll away. It was too late for pulling out to do a damned bit of good and he wanted to stay joined with her a little longer, with his softening length buried inside her and the sticky heat of their pleasure binding them together. He didn't want to think about what came next, or what he would have to do if she lied to him again.

"I'm sorry I ran," she finally whispered. "I saw Adam carrying a cage around to the back of the house and I lost it. I…I was afraid it was for me."

"It was for you." He didn't bother to add that it still might be, depending on her answers to his questions.

"But why?" she asked, her voice breaking. "I thought we had a good time today. I thought we were connecting in a way we hadn't before."

"I agree." He drew back until he could take in her flushed cheeks and blue eyes, still glittering with passion. "That's why I trusted you to remain alone on the porch while I took a phone call. And you rewarded that trust by running away and nearly killing yourself."

Her brows drew together. "And if I hadn't, you would have put me in a cage. What kind of reward is that?"

"I said the cage was for you; I didn't say I was going to put you in it. It was a possibility, not a foregone conclusion."

"Can't you just give a straight answer for once?" she asked. "Is that so difficult?"

"The only thing I've promised you is that I will break you," he said, capturing her wrists and guiding them above her head before pinning them to the sand. "I never promised you truth or affection or anything else."

She held his gaze, her bottom lip trembling. "You're right. You're impossible, but you're right."

"I'm not impossible," he said, shocked to feel desire whispering through his core as she shifted beneath him, her hips sinking deeper into the coarse beach. He wanted to fuck her until he was hard again and they both had more sand in uncomfortable places, but the time for pleasure was through.

He needed answers and he intended to get them. "I'm going to give you a chance to make this better," he said softly. "If you please me, you will sleep in your bed tonight. If you displease me, you sleep in the kennel."

# CHAPTER FOUR

## Jackson

Her eyes widened. "No. I can't. Please, I'm terrified of small spaces."

"Then I suppose you'd better answer my questions honestly." Jackson leaned in until his face hovered inches from hers, close enough for him to see the starbursts of gray surrounding her pupils.

Had Harley's eyes turned into tiny blue and silver suns at their centers? He didn't think so. Not exactly like this, anyway. If he were a gambling man, he would bet this was her sister, Hannah, but he needed to hear it from her own lips.

And then he needed her to tell him why she'd lied.

"What is your name?" he asked, his fingers tightening around her wrists as he relaxed more of his weight on top of her. He wanted her to feel just how vulnerable she was. Vulnerable, exposed, and completely at his mercy.

"My name," she echoed, searching his face. "We're back to this?"

"We are," he said. "But this time I want the truth."

She pulled in a breath and held it for a moment before releasing her words in a rush, "What if you don't believe me?"

"I'll believe you. If you're telling the truth."

"How will you know?"

"I'll know." He would. She had no reason to suspect that he'd discovered her secret. If she confessed the truth now while staring up into his eyes with her body slick around him and the steady thud of her heartbeat echoing through his chest, he would believe her.

"All right, I..." Her tongue slipped out, dampening her lips. "My name is Hannah. Hannah Elisabeth."

He swallowed, keeping his expression impassive, trying not to think too much about all the things he'd done to this woman while laboring under a case of mistaken identity. "Harley is your twin sister."

She nodded, fear and uncertainty swirling in her eyes. "Yes."

"And where is your sister now?" He moved his hands away from her wrists, granting her that slight freedom as a reward for her honesty.

"She's dead," she whispered. "She died in a car accident six years ago."

He closed his eyes. If he didn't, there would be no way he would be able to hide his response. She was telling the truth. Harley was dead and he'd wasted six years of his life hunting a ghost.

Six *fucking* years.

And now here he was, buried balls deep in a stranger he'd been hate fucking for a week, treating her the way he would only have treated his worst enemy.

Throat so tight it felt like it would collapse, Jackson pulled out and rolled away from the woman beneath him. He sat back on his ass in the sand, propping his elbows on his bent knees and dropping his face into his hands, his thoughts worming into such a wicked knot he couldn't pluck a single logical thread from the tangle.

"I'm sorry I lied," Hannah said, the direction of her voice leading him to believe she'd sat up beside him though he still couldn't bring himself to look at her. "I was afraid you wouldn't want me if you knew I wasn't Harley and my aunt and I are in a really hard place. We need the money badly, but after a while I..."

She sighed. "It started to feel so wrong to lie to you, no matter how much is riding on this job. I was going to tell you the truth tonight, at dinner, but when you left the table, I realized I had no way to prove that I had a sister. No pictures or birth certificate or anything. And then I got scared that you wouldn't believe me, so when I saw the—"

"The cage," he supplied numbly. The cage he'd bought for the monster who had slipped through his fingers. Harley was probably rolling around on the steamy floor of hell right now, laughing her ass off at his failure.

But that was all right. He would hunt her there, too. Eventually.

"I'm not sure what she did to you," Hannah said in a careful voice, "but I'm sorry. I'm sure you didn't deserve it. I loved Harley, but I knew her better than anyone. She could be so cruel. She hurt a lot of people who didn't deserve to be hurt. Especially men."

"Why men?" Jackson asked, keeping his eyes closed and his face in his hands. His reality was falling apart, but he wasn't about to let Hannah see him crumble. She might not be his sworn enemy, but he didn't trust her. He didn't trust anyone related to the viper who had put him behind bars.

"I don't know for sure," she said. "I think it was her way of protecting herself. My mother was miserable in her marriage. She had an affair when I was a kid. She was gone for almost a year, and when she came back, Daddy was horrible to her. He treated her like a prisoner, but she never fought back or tried to leave. It was...painful to watch. It scared me and I think it scared Harley even more. She was so afraid of becoming like Mom that she became like Dad, instead, taking what she wanted and hurting before she could be hurt."

Hurting before she could be hurt.

He would *never* have hurt Harley, not back then. And he certainly wouldn't have set off a nuclear bomb in the center of her life the way she had his. The explanation didn't make any sense, but he could tell Hannah was telling the truth as far as she knew it.

But that didn't mean her psychoanalysis of her sister was the entire story. There had to be more to Harley's plot to ruin him, and Hannah was going to help him discover the secrets her sister must have been keeping.

Taking a deep breath, Jackson lifted his head and opened his eyes. Hannah was mirroring his position, her legs curled to her chest and her arms wrapped around her knees, concealing most of her nakedness. They'd spent the past week having boundary-pushing sex and he'd just had her so hard his balls still ached, but he felt like he was looking at a stranger.

He didn't know how to talk to her or be with her and he was too fucked up to cross that bridge just yet. It was better not to think too much about what to do with Hannah, at least not until he had the information he needed.

"Hannah Elisabeth," he said, even her name softer and sweeter in his mouth than Harley's. "Pretty."

Her lashes fluttered as her gaze fell. "Thank you."

"So what is your last name, Hannah Elisabeth?"

She glanced up sharply before dropping her eyes back to the sand and hugging her legs tighter to her chest. "I'd rather not say. If that's okay."

"It's not. I need to know Harley's last name. I already know Garrett, the one she gave me, wasn't it."

Hannah shook her head, her damp, tangled hair moving heavily around her shoulders. "I'm sorry. I can't tell you. My family has enemies. That's why my aunt and I are in hiding. I haven't told anyone my real last name in years."

"What kind of enemies?" he asked, wondering if maybe Hannah wasn't so innocent after all.

"The kind who kill people," she said, her face paling. "Harley's accident wasn't an accident. Someone drove the car she was in off the road. There was reason to believe I would be next so...we ran. It's been just Sybil and me ever since."

"Why would someone want you and your sister dead?"

"I don't know for sure. I have theories, but I'm not ready to share them," she said, her mouth set in a stubborn line. "All I can tell you is that it was nothing Harley or I did. She might not have been innocent, but she'd done nothing to earn her way onto a killer's hit list."

"I understand not being ready to share your secrets with me," he said in a patient voice. "But what you don't understand is that if you don't tell me your last name, you're going to make a new enemy. And I'll be able to get to you a lot easier than anyone else who means you harm."

Hannah's lips parted in shock. "Are you threatening me?"

"I'd rather not, but if you won't give me what I need..."

"B-but I'm not Harley," she sputtered.

"I believe you, and I don't want to punish an innocent woman any more than I have already," he said, muscles tensing, ready to spring after her if she decided to run. "But I need to know the truth. Give me a name and we'll be finished with questions. For now."

Her clever gaze darted to the right before returning to his. She was going to run. He almost hoped she would so he would have something to do with all the frustrated rage coursing through him.

"I can't tell you," she said with another

shake of her head. "If it were only me, it wouldn't matter, but I have to think about Aunt Sybil. I can't put her at risk."

"She won't be in danger," he said. "I won't tell anyone anything about you or your aunt. I just need to know Harley's last name."

Hannah went still, holding his gaze in the fading light. "I can't. Please ask me something else."

"I thought you said you cared about me," Jackson said, unable to keep the hard edge from his voice. "Aren't you supposed to trust the people you care for?"

Her eyes narrowed. "I also said I thought you were out of your mind. So until you prove otherwise, no, I don't trust you. And if you hurt me because I refuse to answer this question, then I will trust you even less and you will *never* get what you want from me."

"Now you're making threats?" he asked in a low, dangerous voice, some primitive part of him gnashing its teeth in rage that she dared to threaten him now, when his entire world had been ripped apart.

"It's not a threat," she whispered. "It's a promise."

He shifted forward, but before he could stand, Hannah sprung to her feet and raced back toward the ocean. He leapt after her, eliminating her brief head start in three large strides. Grabbing her hips, he spun her around and bent low, tipping her over his shoulder.

"Let me go!" she screamed, driving a fist into his back. "Put me down!"

Jackson responded by securing one arm around her thighs, banding them tightly together as he turned and started back up the beach.

He'd given her the chance to play nice.

Now they were going to play his way.

# CHAPTER FIVE

## Hannah

All the way back to the house, Hannah beat Jackson's back with her fists as hard as she could, but it was like his skin had turned to stone along with his heart.

*His heart was always stone.*

*You were a fool to think differently and a fool to let him know you care. He'll just use it against you, another weapon in his crazy, senseless war against a dead woman.*

"I'm not Harley!" Hannah sobbed as Jackson walked around the side of the house, cutting through the garden. She hated the tears filling her eyes. She wasn't sad, she was livid, but apparently her stupid body didn't understand the difference. "I didn't do anything to you! You have no right to punish me."

"I don't need a right. You sold yourself to me," Jackson said in an infuriatingly cold voice. “I can do what I want with the things that I own.”

“I’m not a thing, you bastard,” she said, delivering another hard punch to his muscled back that, again, seemed to have absolutely no effect. “I’m a person. An *innocent* person.”

“No one is innocent,” he said, flipping her upright so suddenly the world spun and her knees buckled.

Before she could even attempt to regain her balance, Jackson’s strong hands gripped her hip and the back of her neck, bending her in half and shoving her forward. She fell onto her hands and knees, knowing as soon as she felt the hard plastic beneath her fingers where she was.

The cage. She was in the cage.

She spun in time to see Jackson slide the lock home and wailed at him through the bars, “No! Let me out! You can’t leave me in here!”

Jackson stood and turned, walking away with that slow, predatory gait of his, as if he couldn’t care less that he’d locked a woman he had just made love to in a dog kennel.

“Stop!” she screamed as he crossed the patio. “I’m not a criminal! I’m not an animal. I don’t deserve to be treated this way!”

He paused with his hand on the sliding glass door and turned, glancing over his shoulder with a pitiless expression on his face. “No one gets what they deserve, Hannah. If you didn't realize that before, you certainly will now."

And then he opened the door and stepped inside, ignoring her shouted, "Wait!"

She sucked in a breath, frightened by the sound that emerged from her parted lips. It was half whimper, half growl, and all crazy. If he left her in here for any length of time, she was going to lose her mind. She could already feel the narrow plastic walls tightening around her, the thin metal web of the bars digging into her skin, slicing her sanity into pieces.

"Let me out," she moaned as she wedged herself into the corner of the kennel, her knees tucked to her chest. "Please, let me out. Please."

But there was no one to hear her beg. The garden beyond the patio was quiet and empty. The only sounds breaking the silence were the wind through the leaves and the insects buzzing and clicking in the soft blue light.

Dusk had fallen on the journey back to the house. Before long, it would be dark and she would be alone until morning. She knew Jackson wasn't coming back for her any time soon. There would be no one to plead with for her freedom until Eva brought her breakfast tray in the morning and for all she knew, she might be denied food until she gave Jackson what he wanted.

"I hate you," she growled, her foot shooting out to kick the opposite wall, sending a shudder through her prison. "I hate you, Jackson! I hate you! Do you hear me? I hate you!"

She screamed until her throat was raw, her eye sockets throbbed, and tears streamed down her cheeks. She screamed until she could have sworn she'd used up all the air in her prison and her head felt light enough to float off her body. She screamed and screamed until darkness fell and the moon rose over the black hulk of the mountain and she was too weak to do anything but curl into a ball on the floor of the cage and cry herself to sleep, pitifully mumbling promises to herself.

She was going to hurt him. She was going to make him sorry he'd done this. She was going to show him that sometimes people *did* get what they deserved and that he wasn't the only one who could become a monster.

By the time she finally began to drift off to sleep—still feeling the full-body crawl of terror only a claustrophobic could fully understand—she had nearly convinced herself that she didn't pity Jackson, let alone love him.

How could she be in love with a man who would hurt her this way?

Nothing he'd done in the past week had been as awful as this. Before today, he hadn't known he had the wrong woman and there had always been pleasure at the end of the pain. The most mind-blowing, heart-wrenching, explosive pleasure of her life, unlike anything she could have imagined until Jackson took her by the hand and led her down his dark path.

But maybe he didn't want to give her pleasure or pain anymore.

She wasn't Harley. She wasn't the woman he wanted. Maybe now that he knew Harley was truly beyond his reach, he wanted answers and nothing more. And maybe, if she broke down and gave him what he was asking for, he'd send her home to Sybil.

The thought should have been a sliver of hope to cling to. Instead, it summoned fresh tears that slid down her already hot, swollen cheeks. She didn't want him to send her away or even to simply let her out of her cage. She wanted him to care the way she cared.

"So stupid, Hannah," she mumbled to the darkness. "You're so fucking stupid."

She'd always heard that love was blind, but apparently it was dumb, as well, and lacking in even the most basic sense of self-respect.

She still loved Jackson, even now, curled on her side with hard plastic digging into her bones, her head full of cotton, and her mouth filled with the sour taste of terror. She still ached for his touch and the feel of his body joining with hers, promising with every brush of skin against skin that she belonged in his arms, and she sensed she would only stop loving him when she began hating herself.

"First thing in the morning," she whispered as her eyes slid closed. She would start to work on hating herself first thing in the morning.

Right now she was too tired for love or hate or anything in between.

# CHAPTER SIX

## Jackson

Jackson locked himself in his room, turning the stereo to a classical station to drown out the sound of Hannah's distant screams. He took a long hot shower, doing his best not to think about anything in particular as he scrubbed the saltwater stickiness from his skin. Afterward, he dressed in silk pajama pants and a cotton tee shirt and sat down to decode a message encrypted on the website his underground contacts used to negotiate prices for his shipments.

If Hannah was still screaming that she hated him an hour later, he couldn't hear it over the soothing piano music, but he would swear he could feel her contempt stinging across the surface of his skin. The hair at the back of his neck stood on end, his jaw ached from being clenched for too long, and his stomach had solidified into a granite slab that weighed down the center of his body. Working was challenging and eating was unthinkable.

When Eva brought him a tray a little after eight, he sent her away, opting for a tumbler of scotch on the rocks instead. He hoped the drink would dull the edges of his anger. But two tumblers later, all it had accomplished was to make it impossible to stop thinking about Hannah, the woman he'd locked in a cage for the crime of not giving him what he wanted.

He was behaving like an infant king, a tyrant given power far greater than his capacity for compassion.

*Her sister destroyed your capacity for compassion and Hannah's purpose is to give you what you want. It doesn't matter that she isn't Harley; you're still paying for her obedience. She knew the rules and she knew she would be punished for disobeying them.*

*She brought every bit of this pain and suffering upon herself.*

That line of defense held until eleven o'clock, when he turned off the lights and slipped between the sheets, only for his mind to stubbornly replay the events of the evening over and over again, keeping him awake and riveted by remembered fear.

He kept seeing Hannah struggling in the waves, reliving the terror that had flooded through him as he realized he might lose her until his heart thudded faster and his arms ached to hold her. All he wanted to do was to press her tight to his chest and assure his anxious mind that she was safe and alive. But she wasn't safe and he doubted any amount of money could convince her to come willingly into his arms. She hated him. As she should. As she should have from the very beginning.

*But she didn't. She cared. And you paid her back with cruelty.*

With a curse, Jackson flung the covers to the end of the bed and rose to pace back and forth on the cool hardwood. A part of him wanted to go to her, to try to make this better, but it was too late. It had always been too late.

Maybe if he'd met Hannah first instead of Harley. Maybe if he'd never become a criminal or learned to take what he wanted and damn the consequences, maybe then he and Hannah could have been something other than enemies. But as things stood, the situation was too fucked up for it to ever be put right again. Harley had made sure of that.

Jackson snatched his phone from the bureau, thumbing back to the picture of the two girls by the lake, feeling something painful flash through his chest at the sight of Hannah's smile. It was the same smile she had as an adult, that sweet, open smile he'd seen in the moments she felt comfortable enough to let down her guard. It was the smile that had made him wonder if there was some way forward for him and Harley, as twisted and crazy as the path might be.

But Hannah wasn't Harley. Harley was dead and Hannah was a stranger he'd known for barely a week.

*She's not a stranger. She's yours.*

*"Fuck me until I know who I belong to."* The memory of her words was enough to make his cock stiffen, but he ignored his body's response. Hannah didn't belong to him and she never would. She deserved better than what he could give her. A broken man was good enough for the woman who had broken him, but he would never be good enough for anyone else.

Ignoring the odd rush of melancholy inspired by the thought, Jackson flipped forward to the letter he hadn't had time to read earlier tonight. Upon closer inspection, he realized it was written in colored pencil and that the contents of the missive weren't as childlike as he'd first assumed. The looping cursive was awkward, but the thoughts the words communicated were unexpectedly eloquent.

*Dear Aunt Syb,*

*I miss you so much! I dream about the lake house every night and wake up sad that I'm not there with you. I wish it were already next summer. Don't tell them I told, but Mom is still as sad as when we left and Dad is always at work. Sometimes I wonder if they wish they didn't have kids, but I'm probably wrong. I guess I'm just cranky because Nanny Hammond is awful.*

*She punishes us BOTH every time Harley does something bad!*

*Harley says it's because Nanny is too dumb to tell us apart, but I think she does it to try to make Harley feel guilty so she'll stop getting into trouble. But Harley never feels guilty and at this rate I'm never going to get to go to my rock-climbing lesson again. It's always taken away as a punishment.*

*It almost makes me want to break the rules just so there's a reason for being punished, but my heart gets all jumpy just thinking about doing things I'm not supposed to do. The closest I got to being bad was sneaking into Nanny's room and putting leaves in her underwear drawer. When Harley found out, she teased me for being a baby. She said she would have put mice or cockroaches in there instead. And she probably would have.*

*She's so angry all the time, Aunt Syb. She's not the same as she is when we're at your house. So when we come home I miss you* and *her, even though she's right here beside me.*

*Does that sound crazy?*

*I hope not. Sometimes I'm scared of ending up like Mom. Nanny says depression is a disease, so we can't blame Mom for it. And I don't, but sometimes, when I'm sad, I wonder if I'm catching depression, too.*

*But I know I wouldn't catch it at the lake house, Aunt Syb. I know I would be happy and could grow up to be a good person, like you. I just want to be happy and good and not to be scared or sad all the time. That's why I'm writing to ask you to please,*

*please, please ask Daddy to let me come live with you. I know he'll say yes if you ask.*

*And then I could go to school there and help you whenever your arthritis is giving you trouble. I promise I will be the very best kid ever and never let you down. Cross my heart and hope to die!*

*Much love and hoping to see you soon,*

*Hannah*

Jackson set the phone back on the bureau, his head bowed and his throat tight. It had been a long time since he'd felt anything close to this fierce sense of empathy and he wasn't sure what to do with the emotion swelling inside of him.

No child should have to feel so scared and alone. His childhood home had been cold and loveless, but at least he hadn't been constantly punished for a sibling's misbehavior. And he'd gotten out, scheming his way to freedom when he wasn't much older than Hannah had been when she wrote this letter. It made him want to reach through time, scoop up that lonely, neglected little girl, and find a way to get her to the aunt who loved her.

But he couldn't rescue the child Hannah had been. The best he could do was save the woman she'd become.

Before he'd made the conscious choice to move, he was through the bedroom door, striding through the darkened great room and down the hall toward the master suite. Inside, the air still smelled like Hannah, a sweet and sexy smell he knew would haunt him long after she was gone, but he didn't pause to draw it in.

Now that he'd made the decision, he couldn't get to her fast enough.

He was already going to be too late. Too late to spare her another ugly memory of being punished for her sister's crimes, too late to reward her loyalty to the aunt she loved so much or to show her that he wasn't completely rotten inside. There was still some healthy tissue hidden away in the diseased corridors of his heart. She had shown him that, but unfortunately for the both of them, the discovery had come too late.

## CHAPTER SEVEN

### Jackson

Outside on the patio, Jackson glanced down through the web of bars on the roof of the kennel to see Hannah asleep, curled into a pitiful ball in one corner of her cage.

A sharp, slightly sour smell rose from her body, sending a fresh wave of self-loathing oozing through his chest.

He knew that smell. It was the smell of terror and captivity, made familiar from his first days in prison when his clothes had been constantly damp with sweat despite the chill in his cell.

It had taken a week for his body to adapt to living in a cage, but his mind had never adjusted. Once you've known what it's like to have your freedom unjustly taken away, it's impossible to recover.

Trust, faith, hope, and all the other fragile

things that give life deeper meaning become impossible, locked away in a room inside of you that has no key.

He knew from experience something like this could never be undone. Hannah would never forget being caged for the crime of trusting the wrong person. She'd only been in the kennel for a few hours, but she would bear the scars of this encounter for the rest of her life.

Bracing himself for the worst, Jackson knelt to peer into the cage, where Hannah's skin glowed like moonlight reflecting on the ocean. She was beautiful—the curve of her hip poetry in the darkness that surrounded her—but he still wished he'd given her clothes. It was warm enough that she shouldn't be cold, but her nudity added to the cruelty of her punishment.

He could imagine how vulnerable she must have felt in those moments before she fell asleep when she was lying naked and alone inside a cage meant for a dog.

She'd told him that she cared about him, and in exchange, he'd treated her like an animal.

She was right to hate him.

Hatred was all he deserved.

"Hannah," he said, knowing putting this off until morning wouldn't make it any easier. "Hannah, wake up. I'm here to let you out."

She moaned and shifted in her sleep, but her eyes remained closed.

"Hannah," he repeated in a firmer voice. "Wake up, Hannah."

She woke with a start, her head snapping up, sending her tangled hair flying. With her curls obscuring her features he couldn't see her face, but he knew the moment she saw him.

She cringed away with a sound of disgust, pressing herself against the wall of the kennel and drawing her knees to her chest.

"What do you want?" she asked, her voice low and hoarse from screaming.

"I'm here to let you out." He flipped the latch, letting the gate swing open, but Hannah didn't move. She remained in her corner, making it clear she'd rather stay in the dog crate than move a centimeter closer to him.

"What do you want?" she demanded again, voice rising sharply. "*Why* are you letting me out?"

"I thought you might want a shower," he said as he backed away from the kennel, knowing it was the wrong thing to say when a bark of laughter burst from Hannah's lips.

"A shower," she repeated as she crawled through the gate and stood shakily, her arms clasped across her chest. "You thought I might want a *shower*."

Jackson sighed, but she cut him off before he could find something less ridiculous to say.

"No, I don't want a shower." She lunged forward suddenly, sobbing as her palms struck his ribs. "I want to hurt you, you twisted son of a bitch!" She shoved him again, sending him staggering back a step. "I want to lock you naked in a cage and let you know what it feels like to have the walls closing in and your skin crawling off of your body."

Jackson lifted his hands into the air, the gesture of surrender resonating in some deep, primal part of his brain.

He suddenly realized there was only one way to show Hannah how profoundly he regretted what he'd done. Slowly, he reached for the bottom of his shirt, pulling it over his head before letting it fall to the ground.

"What are you doing?" Hannah edged back a step, wariness in her tone.

"You said you wanted me naked." He could sense where her thoughts were headed and how little she wanted him to touch her, but this wasn't about sex.

It was about being as vulnerable as she was, something she'd realize when she saw his cock limp between his legs.

He shoved his pants to the ground and stepped out of them before kneeling on the hard stone at her feet. "There's a crop in the bedside table drawer. You should get it. If you beat me with your hands, you'll hurt yourself."

He watched her bare toes curl against the

stone, but didn't lift his eyes from the ground. He couldn't stand to look at her right now.

Seeing how close she was to a breakdown and knowing he was the one who had driven her there was even more painful than he'd imagined it would be.

"You want me to beat you?" she asked.

"I'm too big to fit in the kennel," Jackson said practically. "A beating would be a reasonable substitute, but if you'd rather punish me some other way, that's up to you. Whatever you decide, you have my full cooperation."

"Why?" she said. "Look at me, Jackson."

He kept his chin tucked close to his chest. "You know why."

"Jackson, look at me," she repeated. "Let me see your face."

Slowly, he tilted his head, meeting her gaze in the dim light.

The moon was hiding behind the thick clouds that had moved in not long after sunset, but there was enough illumination to see the way her eyes glittered with a mixture of rage and suspicion. It was clear that she would never trust him again, not even the small amount that she had before.

The knowledge made his chest feel heavy and his voice flat when he said, "Because I deserve it."

"What did you do to deserve it," she pressed, refusing to let him off easy. "Tell me what you did wrong."

"Once I knew who you were, the ugliness should have stopped," he said. "I never should have fucked you on the beach or dragged you back here against your will. And I sure as hell shouldn't have put you in the kennel."

"Then why did you?" she asked, shaking her head as if he were a puzzle she would never be able to make sense of.

But there was no puzzle.

He was a simple creature, a simple monster, and after all he'd put her through she deserved to know his creation story.

"Because I'm a twisted son of a bitch. Like you said. And I'm never going to be anything else." He took a deep breath. "It started six years ago when your sister filed a report with the military police accusing me of rape."

He let the rest of the story spill out, every detail of that summer that had started out golden and ended in a nightmare he couldn't wake from, no matter how many times he'd insisted that he had never touched Harley in anger.

"I don't know how she did it," he continued. "In the video of her interview with the police she was covered in bruises, but the last time I saw her she was fine. There wasn't a mark on her. I saw every inch of her." He swallowed hard. "We slept together and I told her that I loved her for the first time. She said she loved me, too, and...I believed it. I believed her."

His lip curled, disgust for the fool he'd been making his skin crawl. "Later, I found out that she'd been killed later that same night, on her way to elope with my best friend, days after framing me for a crime I didn't commit. I was sentenced to eighteen months in a military prison and dishonorably discharged from the Marines. My family hasn't spoken to me since I was taken in for questioning."

Hannah's breath rushed out. "Jesus." She sat down across from him, her arms still folded at her chest. "I thought it was something like that, but I never... I had no idea that you'd gone to prison. Or that the man who was in the car with her was your friend."

"Don't pity me," he said in a brittle voice. "That's not why I told you the truth. I told you so you'll understand that I have nothing to offer you except the chance to even the score. Now go get the crop."

"I don't want to get the crop," she said, sounding exasperated. "You know, there's such a thing as an apology, Jackson. Where you say you're sorry for something you've done and the other person says you're forgiven."

"I don't deserve to be forgiven."

Her gaze softened. "Then I guess this time it's lucky for you that people don't always get what they deserve." She reached out, laying a hand on his arm. "I believe that you're sorry. And I forgive you."

He shook his head, fighting to swallow as a wave of emotion tightened his throat. "You can't."

"You don't get to tell me what to do," she said stubbornly. "That's not the place we're in right now. I want to forgive you, so I will. And I hope you'll forgive me, too."

"There's nothing to forgive," he said, sitting back on his heels, the knot in his throat even worse than it had been before.

"Yes, there is." She moved closer, taking his hand in both of hers. "I played my part in the confusion you've been feeling for so long. I didn't realize it, but..." Her fingers tightened around his palm. "That wasn't Harley you were with the night you climbed through her window, Jackson. It was me."

He glanced up but was too stunned to form a response.

"I tried to tell you," Hannah said, anxiety creeping into her tone. "But you thought I was playing along with the game. And then, after the first time we were together when I had the chance to tell you it had all been a horrible mistake, I...I didn't want to."

Her gaze fell to their joined hands. "Because it wasn't horrible. It was wonderful. And that's why I smiled when you took the blindfold off. Because I'd been hoping to see you again for so long, even though I knew it was wrong, and that it was Harley you cared about, not me."

"I...I can't..." He trailed off, still not knowing what to say, only that so many things finally made sense now.

Not just the bruises, but the way Harley had seemed so naturally submissive that night, almost like a different person.

It was because she *had* been a different person.

She'd been Hannah.

It was Hannah who had made him believe he and Harley had a future.

It had been Hannah all along.

"Can you forgive me?" she asked.

"There's nothing to forgive," he repeated, hoping she could tell that he meant it. "I should have known the difference. If I hadn't drunk half a bottle of scotch before I came through Harley's window, I would have. It was my fault as much as yours."

"Not really," she said, her lips lifting on one side. "But thank you."

"God, Hannah, don't thank me." He tried to pull his hand away, but she held tight. "I'm glad you told me the truth, but I'm not that man anymore. I couldn't be, even if I tried."

"I don't believe you." She drew his hand toward her, guiding it to rest, palm down, on her chest.

His fingers fit neatly between her bare breasts and the feel of her soft, warm flesh had the usual effect on his body. His cock didn't care that he hated himself. His cock only cared that he could have Hannah's breast cupped in his hand with a shift of his wrist.

But he refused to indulge the urge.

Sex was no longer an option, not if he were truly sorry for the things he'd done.

"Don't do this to yourself," he said, his voice rough. "I'm sorry for what I did tonight and all the other nights, but I can't promise I won't do something like that again." He grimaced. "Or something worse. I'm not safe for you."

"Who said I wanted safe?" she asked, leaning closer. "I'm not a fool, Jackson. I know you're dangerous and I'm not looking for any big promises. All I need is one thing."

"What's that?" Her nipples brushed against his chest, sending heat spreading through his core.

He clenched his jaw, fighting to keep from reaching for her.

"Tell me that you care," she said in her soft, sexy voice. "Even if it's only a little. Because if you can care a little, then you can learn to care a lot. And maybe someday you'll even learn to let yourself be happy."

Jackson pressed his lips together, but it did nothing to stop the ache spreading through his chest. He didn't deserve this; he didn't deserve her, but he couldn't hide from how much he wanted what she was offering.

He was broken and twisted and wrong

inside, but when Hannah touched him it felt right, *he* felt right in a way he hadn't in so long.

Not since that night in Harley's bed when he'd unknowingly slept with the wrong sister.

"Tell me you care, Jackson," she whispered, kissing first one corner of his mouth and then the other. "I know you do. And I know you want me as much as I want you."

"I want you so much," he said, his eyes sliding closed. "I want you like my next breath, but I'll hurt you, Hannah. I know I will and I don't want to."

"Why don't you want to?" she asked as she reached down, her cool fingers closing around his erection, stroking him with a gentle insistence that sent longing and grief flooding through him in equal measure.

She had him right where she wanted him. He couldn't deny her though he knew this wouldn't end well.

It never did when Beauty fell in love with the Beast.

"Because I care about you." His eyes opened as his fingers closed around her wrist, stopping her mid-stroke. He stared deep into her big eyes, willing her to see what a bad idea this was. "But this isn't a fairy tale. In real life, the monster doesn't get better. In real life, the monster drags you down to hell with him and you burn there."

"You make me burn, that's true." Her lips

twisted in a wry smile. "Which reminds me that I have a favor to ask, sir."

"What's that?" he asked, not sure whether to feel grateful or terrified that she was taking them back onto familiar ground.

Things between them would never be the same.

She could call him "sir" a thousand times, but he was vulnerable now and they both knew it. They might be using the same pieces, but this was a whole other game, one he wasn't sure he remembered how to play.

"I would like a safe word," she said. "People like us usually have those, right?"

"They do," he said, mesmerized by the feel of her fingertips teasing across his palm. "Though I'm not sure there are other people exactly like us."

She shrugged one shoulder. "That doesn't have to be a bad thing."

He made a non-committal sound. This was all bad, but it was hard to concentrate on good and bad when she was naked in the moonlight, looking up at him like he was all she needed to get through the night. "So what's your safe word, sunshine?"

She cocked her head. "No more princess?"

"Sunshine suits you better."

She nodded, her lashes fluttering as she swallowed. "See? You can be sweet," she said, pushing on before he could assure her that he was as far from sweet as a man could get. "And my safe word is cheese biscuits. I'd like to see you stay mean and growly when I'm shouting cheese biscuits in your ear."

Against all odds, a smile stretched across his face. "Cheese biscuits? Those are the words that make you feel safe?"

"What's safer than a fluffy biscuit, covered in melted cheese?" she asked with mock seriousness. "That's practically the definition of safety."

"You're funny," he said, warmth spreading through his chest.

"I'm not funny." She shifted her weight as she shook her head slowly back and forth. "I'm a very serious person, and I've got a serious problem."

He lifted a brow. "What's that?"

"I think it's best if I show you, sir." She held his gaze as she guided his hand between her legs. As his fingers slid through the slick folds of her sex, a ragged sigh escaped his lips.

When he'd come out here, he'd been certain he would never touch her this way again. And he wouldn't have if she weren't the person she was, a generous, gentle, unbelievably strong woman who had looked into the darkest corners of his soul and refused to be scared away.

And because she was who she was, he could be something better, at least for the night.

"You won't need your safe word this time,"

he said, pressing one finger deep into the well of her heat, relishing the way she spread her thighs, welcoming him in. "There won't be any games tonight. It will just be you and me."

"Should I still call you 'sir'?" she asked, anxiety flickering across her features.

"Don't be afraid," he said. "I can't make you any promises about the future, but I swear there won't be any pain tonight."

"But sometimes pain is easier, isn't it?" she said, proving she understood the game far better than most people who had only just begun to play.

"It can be," he agreed, withdrawing his fingers from her slickness and taking her by the hand. "Pain gives you a place to hide. But I can't hide tonight. I'm not in the right head-space. So if you'd rather go to bed alone, I understand."

"That's the last thing I want." She squeezed his hand. "Take me to bed, Jackson. If you're not afraid, I'm not, either."

*Who said I'm not afraid?*

He *was* afraid. So afraid.

Of her, of himself, of the trust in her eyes and the affection in her touch. He would betray her trust and affection. He was certain of it, but still he held on tight to her hand as he led her through the sliding doors toward the bed.

He held tight because somewhere deep

inside of himself, a voice whispered that maybe it wasn't too late.

He could never go back, but maybe there was a way forward, as long as he kept his eyes on this woman who believed that he could be something more than a monster.

# CHAPTER EIGHT

## Hannah

Pulse racing with a heady combination of desire and fear, Hannah stretched out on the bed, waiting with bated breath for Jackson to lie down beside her. This shouldn't be more frightening than being spanked, punished, or locked in a cage, but it was. The look in his eyes, as he gazed down at her, was the scariest thing she'd ever seen.

He was so vulnerable, adrift and directionless, with all his carefully constructed armor falling away. He reminded her of a wounded predator, made more dangerous by the knowledge that his defenses were weakened. But he was also utterly captivating.

For the first time since she'd come into his keeping, she glimpsed the man she'd met that night in her sister's bed, the man capable of trust and affection. He'd been wounded by betrayal and smothered by rage, but he was still there, nearly within her reach, and she didn't want to do anything to scare him away.

As Jackson eased onto the mattress beside her, she was shocked to realize that she felt like the Dominant one tonight. The responsibility for his emotional well-being lay heavy on her shoulders, but she could handle the weight. She was stronger than she'd imagined she could be. Jackson had taught her that. He'd shown her the strength in submission and the core of steel that ran through her softness.

And tonight she would use her strength to begin leading him out of the darkness before it was too late.

"You're beautiful," he said, his palm skimming up her stomach to cup her breast reverently in his hand. "Have I told you how beautiful you are?"

"Yes. I think stunning was another word you used," she said, knowing it was exactly the word he'd used. She would never forget a single word he'd said to her, this man who had captured her imagination, her heart, and everything in between. "You're pretty stunning yourself."

"I'm glad I please you," he said, rolling her nipple between his fingers, sending a sweet ache flooding through her core.

"You do more than please me." She pushed gently at his shoulders until he rolled onto his back. "You drive me crazy." She leaned down, holding his gaze as she pressed a kiss to the center of his chest. "I've never wanted anyone the way I want you."

She moved higher, trailing kisses up his neck until she reached his mouth, where she let her lips hover a whisper above his. "Am I allowed to kiss you anywhere I want now?"

"Anywhere you want, sunshine," he said, the pet name making her heart turn over. The way he said that word spoke louder than any promise. When he said *sunshine*, she heard *I love you*.

Someday soon, she hoped he would hear it too, and realize maybe they weren't so far from the fairy tale, after all.

"Everything is going to be okay," she said, cupping his scruffy cheek in her hand as she addressed the unspoken doubt in his eyes. "It will, Jackson. I promise."

And then she kissed him and he kissed her back, his tongue slipping into her mouth and his arms wrapping tight around her. The kiss was as hot as any they'd shared, but it was also richer, deeper, an exploration of new territory and an offering of something more than their physical bodies. There was more than hunger in his touch as he cupped her breasts in his hands, kneading and caressing her sensitive skin until she was dizzy. There was more than a desire for release in the way he urged her thighs apart and pressed his erection tight to the slickness between her legs.

She could sense the emotion simmering beneath his touch and the longing for a union that thrummed through his veins. It was the same longing that swelled inside her, filling her with warmth, crowding out the last of her fear.

"I need you so much," she mumbled against his lips. "I need to feel you inside me."

"Condom." He reached for the bedside table, but she took his hand, guiding it back to her breast.

"No, I want you bare," she said, grinding her slickness up and down his rigid length. "It isn't the right time for a baby and we've already gone without a condom once today. Once more won't hurt."

"I know we did," he said, pinching her nipples. "But I didn't realize it until after. I wasn't thinking." He groaned softly as she circled her hips, coating his cock with more of her wet heat. "That's what you do to me, Hannah. You make me forget to think."

"Good." She reached between them, positioning him at her entrance. "You think too much."

She dropped her hips, taking him inside her, inch by glorious inch. She'd never been on top with him before and relished the new way he filled her. His engorged erection took up every inch of space until there was a hint of pain as she sank down the final inch, fitting her hips to his.

But it was sweet pain, the kind that only drove her desire higher.

She moaned as she began to move, gliding up and down his shaft as he dropped his head, suckling her nipple into his mouth. His hands squeezed her hips, sending fresh waves of need coursing through her body and a ringing sensation vibrating through her cells. She felt like a tuning fork finding the perfect pitch, a meditation bell summoning the chaos of the world into perfect harmony, and was suffused with a sense of rightness that swept away the last clinging cobwebs of doubt.

There was no longer any question in her mind—this was where she was meant to be. She belonged with this man. She was born to share his bed, warm his heart, and climb out of hell by his side. It was as close to a moment of utter truth as she'd ever experienced, and she had to know if he felt it too.

"Wait. I need to see you. Please." Fighting the pleasure cresting within her, she squirmed until he released her nipple and lay back, his breath coming fast.

"Just don't ask me to stop," he said, thrusting sharply into her core, his cock stroking so deep it drew a gasp from her throat. "I can't stop. I need you so much. So fucking much." A pained expression flashed across his face that she understood completely.

It was painful to get this close, so close there was nothing but a fraying thread keeping you from losing yourself and being eaten alive by need for the person in your arms. It was heaven and hell mixed together, but better for it.

Darkness made the light shine brighter, pain made pleasure that much sweeter, and what was the point of angels if not to save beautiful devils like Jackson Hawke.

"I won't give up on you," she whispered, holding his gaze as she caught his rhythm, riding him with sensuous rolls of her hips, building the fire already raging between them. "I won't ever give up."

His grip on her hips tightened until his fingertips dug into her flesh. "Hannah."

It was only her name, but it carried so much. It bore his fear, his sadness, and his pain. It held his certainty that they were doomed to fail and the fragile hope that maybe his heart wasn't dead and buried after all.

"It's not too late." She leaned down until her hair fell around their faces, providing a safe place to say dangerous things. "I love you. Every part of you."

He answered her with a kiss, groaning into her mouth as he fisted a hand in her hair and rolled them both over, reversing their positions. As soon as he took control, he made the most of it, grinding against her clit until she was trembling all over and gasping into his mouth.

"Yes," she breathed, eyes sliding closed as he took her higher. Higher and higher until there was nothing but light and bliss and the heaven of finding where she fit. Just right.

"Come, Hannah," Jackson said, his teeth scraping against her throat. "Come for me, beautiful."

She obeyed with a ragged cry, her inner walls pulsing around him as he gripped her hips and thrust into her clutching heat, stroking into her with deep, languid thrusts that threatened to send her tumbling over a second time. But she clenched her jaw and clung to his shoulders, fighting the second wave, not wanting to go again without his permission. They weren't playing games tonight, but her pleasure still belonged to him.

*Every part of you belongs to him. For better or for worse, you're his. Only his.*

"I'm yours," she gasped, threading her fingers into his hair. "Yours. God, yes. Please. Please!"

Jackson's tempo grew faster until he was driving inside of her with a wild abandon that let her know how close he was to the edge. "I'm going to come," he said, his voice strained. "Come with me. Come with me."

"Yes," she said, wrapping her legs tighter

around his waist as his rhythm faltered. "I'm coming. Right...now."

She groaned as his cock jerked inside of her, the feel of his heat scalding her inner walls sending her spiraling a second time. She clung to him as the waves of bliss swept across her skin again and again, wringing sensation from her body until movement was impossible and she and Jackson lay tangled together on the sweat-damp sheets, his body pinning hers to the mattress as they remembered how to breathe.

He was heavy, but she loved the feel of him relaxed on top of her like this. In the quiet moments after release, Jackson was finally at peace. It didn't last long, but maybe someday it would.

Maybe one night, not too long from now, they would fall asleep with their bodies entwined and wake up in the morning with nothing between them but shared happiness. The road to that place wouldn't be smooth or easy, but right now, with the feel of his heart beating in time with hers making her bones hum with contentment, she believed they could get there.

As Jackson rolled onto his back and drew her into his arms, clearly intending to spend the night, she began to believe a little more. And when he kissed her forehead and said, "Sweet dreams, sunshine," her chest filled with so much hope that her heart ached with a fierce, sweet wanting.

The sins of the past didn't matter. They would find a way to put it all behind them and move on. She was sure of it.

# CHAPTER NINE

## Hannah

Hannah drifted into a sleep more peaceful than any in recent memory and dreamt of an afternoon on the beach with Jackson.

They made love in the shade of a palm tree and fed each other slices of pineapple before running into the ocean and making love again amidst the waves.

It was such a lovely dream that she woke up smiling, determined to make her dream a reality.

She rolled over, blinking in the early morning light, a little disappointed to see the rumpled covers beside her empty.

But wherever Jackson had gone he would be back. And when he returned, she would talk him into spending the day at the beach with her.

It would be like a first date.

The thought made her smile, a goofy grin she was glad Jackson wasn't around to see. She knew he still had his fears and doubts, but after the way they had made love last night, she had a hard time holding on to her own. Still, they would have to move forward slowly, and it was too early in the process for love struck grins and humming on her way to the bathroom.

But as she padded into the bathroom to wash up, she couldn't stop an airy tune from vibrating up her throat to her lips.

And when she emerged wrapped in a towel to find her clothes from yesterday freshly washed and laid out on the bed, she let out a blissful sigh, startling Eva, who was depositing her breakfast tray on the table by the window.

"Good morning, Eva," she said, dancing across the room. "Isn't it a beautiful day?"

"Good morning," Eva said with a shy smile. "Mr. Hawke ask for me to bring these special. For you. Special breakfast from him."

"Thank you so much." Hannah glanced down, warmth spreading through her as she realized what was on the tray.

On the delicate china plate sat two steaming biscuits, each cut in half and topped with a different kind of cheese.

Cheese biscuits.

He'd had her safe word delivered for breakfast.

It was funny, sweet, and weirdly romantic,

and she could barely contain the giddy cry of delight threatening to burst from her lips. She was so touched that it took a beat for her to notice the piece of paper with her name written on it tucked beneath the edge of the plate.

It took even longer for her to make sense of the message written inside...

*Dear Hannah,*

*I never thought I'd experience something like last night again.*

*You touched parts of me I was certain no longer existed, but there are other parts that are unreachable, even by a spirit as lovely as yours.*

*That's why I have to leave.*

*I am not now, nor will I ever be, worthy of your affection. I could try for a hundred years, but I would still fall short of what you deserve.*

*I can't be the man you want me to be. I am incapable of love, but I do care enough about you to do what's right.*

*Adam will fly me to my destination this morning and return this afternoon to take you home. The remainder of your fee will be deposited in your account by close of business today.*

*Thank you for your goodness.*

*And your forgiveness.*

*Both mean more than you know.*

*Yours,*

*Jackson*

She read the note through three times before the truth penetrated.

When it did, she dropped the paper and spun toward the bed, dropping her towel and pulling on her clothes, heedless of the fact that Eva was still in the room to see her naked.

A glance at the clock on the bedside table said it was only six fifteen. If she hurried, she might be able to catch Jackson before he left.

She couldn't let him slip away without a fight, not when they were so close to finding forever.

On some level, he must know they were meant to be or he wouldn't have signed the note the way he did.

Subconsciously, he knew that he belonged

to her and she belonged to him. Now, she just had to convince the rest of the stubborn man she loved that the last thing he should be doing is running away.

As soon as her hiking boots were tied, Hannah stood and turned to pin Eva with a stern look. "I need to go to Mr. Hawke. Is there someone who can drive me to the airstrip?"

Eva shook her head, but before she could respond a deep voice spoke from the door.

"I'll take her, Mama." The dark-eyed boy who had warned her about Jackson motioned for her to follow him. "They left a few minutes ago. We can catch up if we go now."

Hannah hurried toward the door, skin prickling with relief. "Thank you so much. I promise you won't get in trouble. I won't let him punish you."

"I'm not worried about being punished," the man said, starting down the hallway toward the front of the house. "My name is Dominic."

"Hannah," she said, then shook her head. "I'm sorry, you know that. I'm just... I'm a little flustered this morning. I can't believe he left like this."

"It might be for the best," Dominic said, slowing as they reached the great room and turning back to face her.

His almost black-brown eyes flicked to check the corners of the room before he added in a whisper. "I can have a plane here in an hour to get you out. I've got a pilot waiting on Moorea. All I have to do is make a phone call."

Hannah blinked in surprise, but her mind quickly connected the dots. "You're the one who sent the note saying that you would help me."

Dominic nodded, continuing in a low voice, "I work for your father. He's sent money to help you get resettled. As soon as we're on board the plane, I'll make contact with your aunt. She can meet us at the airport. That will give you about an hour to decide where you want to go next."

"Where to go next," Hannah repeated, her heart beating faster. "You mean where to hide next."

"I can't say for certain, but your enemies might already know where you are," he said, confirming her fears. "And if they do, they will come for you. Soon."

"So Jackson isn't one of them," she said, relief coursing through her when he shook his head. She hadn't thought Jackson was one of the people hunting her family, but it was good to have confirmation of the fact.

"No," Dominic said. "But that doesn't mean he isn't dangerous. The sooner you're away from him, the better."

"Do you know who wants to hurt my family?" she asked, ignoring his advice. "Who are they? And why do they—"

"Who and why doesn't matter. All that matters is that they want you dead." The matter-of-fact way he said the words made them even more chilling. "You and every other heir to your father's fortune and they won't stop until the job is finished."

Hannah shook her head, the need to get to Jackson warring with her fear.

And mistrust.

That was there too, bubbling beneath the surface.

Dominic was saying all the right things, but he could be lying. He could be a wolf in sheep's clothing, pretending to be her friend until he had her isolated on a plane with nowhere to run.

"How do I know I can trust you?" she asked.

"I've worked for your father for almost ten years," he said, proving, if he were telling the truth, that he was much older than he looked.

Her eyes narrowed.

"I've been watching you for the past three years and you never knew I was there," he continued. "If I'd wanted to hurt you, I could have done so a thousand times. I could have killed you while you were sleeping in your yellow canopy bed or while you hiked by the waterfalls behind your house or when you went to pick lemons with your friends at the grove up the side of the mountain."

Hannah took a step back, his intimate knowledge of her life at the bed and breakfast making her skin crawl.

He really had been watching her.

But that didn't prove he was one of the good guys, especially considering who he was working for here on the island.

No matter how much she cared about Jackson, or how much she believed he could change, she knew what he was. He was a criminal who had intended to do bad things to her and he had been careful to hire people he could trust not to interfere with his plans.

People who wouldn't lift a finger to help her when she screamed for help or begged for mercy and somehow Dominic had found his way onto that list.

"How did you get this job?" she asked. "You and your mother? If she is your mother."

"She is," Dominic said. "But I'm not at liberty to reveal more information."

Hannah smiled, but she was far from amused. "So I'm just supposed to trust a man who's working for an admitted criminal, no questions asked?"

"You trust *him*," he said, gaze hardening. "You're ready to chase down the man who locked you in a cage and beg him to stay with you. You think that's a better idea?"

"You don't miss much, do you?" she

muttered, glancing toward the lanai, where she and Jackson had almost had a lovely meal.

But they hadn't.

Instead, she'd run from him, he'd pursued her, and she'd spent the next twelve hours swinging from intense hatred of the man to confessing her love for him as their bodies came together in the dark.

But between love and hate only one had felt true and now only one decision felt like the right one.

It didn't matter if she was crazy; she had to go to Jackson.

She had to see him again and convince him that it wasn't time to say goodbye.

"I'm going to the airstrip to see Jackson, and I'm going alone," she said, turning back to Dominic with her fists balled at her sides, ready to fight him if he tried to stop her. "How do I get there?"

"There's a golf cart parked in the driveway with the keys in the ignition," he said, not seeming surprised by her decision.

But then, Dominic didn't seem like the type of person who was surprised by much.

"Follow the road until it forks and take a left," he continued. "You'll see the airstrip about four miles down on your right."

Hannah moved to go but stopped when Dominic called after her—

"Are you going to tell him who I am? If so,

I need to get my mother to safety before you get back."

She turned, cocking her head as she studied his guarded expression. "Do you trust my word that much?"

His eyes softened. "I told you. I've been watching you. I know who you are, Hannah. I know you're a good person and that you deserve better than a *canto cabron* who has to hurt his lover to feel like a man."

Hannah frowned but didn't bother contradicting him or trying to explain the way Jackson could make pain feel like pleasure.

It was none of Dominic's business and she didn't have time to waste with explanations.

Besides, she didn't care what Dominic or anyone else thought of her or Jackson; she only cared about getting to the man she loved before it was too late.

"I won't tell him anything about you or your mother," she said. "I give you my word."

"And I give you mine that I'll do my best to protect you until you're ready to leave," he said. "Let me know when you decide to get out. If I'm not able to help you, I'll find someone who can."

"Well, thank you," she said, backing toward the front door. "I appreciate that."

"I'll do my best, Hannah," he said, his brow furrowing with concern. "But I can't assure your safety here. Watch yourself. If you see something suspicious, run first and ask questions later."

She shivered, the fear in this no-nonsense man's voice bringing the danger she was in home in a visceral way.

If she valued her life over all else, she would run now, and figure out a way to reach Jackson once she was safely hidden away.

But she had learned that there were more important things than safety. She would rather spend a year living dangerously with Jackson than another twenty years in hiding, watching the world pass her by.

She was done hiding and waiting for her life to begin.

From now on she would fight for what she wanted, no matter what or who stood in her way.

## CHAPTER TEN

### Jackson

Jackson leaned back in the cool leather seat, watching through the jet's window as Adam and the attendant who manned the field's small tower during daylight hours made their way down the tar-streaked pavement, dragging fallen limbs and other debris from the airstrip.

The sad state of the runway was costing him precious time, but for once he didn't mind. The delay allowed him to continue to breathe the same air she breathed for a little longer, to spend another twenty minutes replaying every moment of his time with Hannah.

Once the plane took off, he would put her out of his mind and move on, but for now he indulged himself, drifting from one memory to the next, summoning an ache deep in his chest.

It was like pushing on a bruise—hurtful, but strangely gratifying. For the first time in years, he was capable of feeling something other than hate. He felt pain, regret, and a sad, hopeless affection for the woman he'd left sleeping so peacefully in the early morning light.

Her face had looked childlike this morning, her features so relaxed it was clear she didn't have a care in the world. And that's why he had to care for her. Leaving was the best—the only—way to do that, but he couldn't help wishing things were different. He wished that he could promise her something other than pain or at the very least have said a proper goodbye.

But he hadn't trusted himself not to weaken. Just the smell of her was enough to make him want to stay. She wouldn't have had to say a word.

For a moment, he thought his memory had conjured up the salt and honey scent of her, sending it drifting through the plane's open door, overpowering the smell of jet fuel and jungle, but then he heard footsteps on the metal stairs leading up to the cabin.

A moment later Hannah appeared in the doorway, backlit by the early morning light, her hair wild around her shoulders and her breath coming fast, making him wonder if she'd run all the way here.

He wouldn't put it past her.

She was stubborn, determined—a force to be reckoned with. He knew all of that about her. He knew her better than he'd known anyone in years. He also knew that this goodbye was going to be even harder than he'd imagined.

"Tell me you didn't run all the way from the house," he said because he didn't dare say anything else. He couldn't apologize for leaving or give her any reason to believe his resolve was weakening.

"I found a golf cart with the keys in the ignition and I stole it," she said, arms braced on either side of the entrance. "I read your note."

"Then why are you here?" he asked, his tone cool.

"Because that note is bullshit." She stood straighter. "And you know it. I don't need you to protect me from you or anything else. All I need is you. With me. Please, Jackson, I—"

"That's why you nearly drowned yesterday? Because you don't need protection from your own bad ideas?" He turned back to the window. "Go back to the house, Hannah. This is over."

"No, it is not over." She moved to stand in front of him, but he feigned great interest in the work of the men outside. "I love you. And I know you love me, even if you're too scared to admit it."

He glanced up at her, keeping his face

fixed in an indifferent mask. "I don't love you; I'm scared for you. But as soon as this plane takes off, I won't be scared of anything. I will cease to think of you and by the end of the month, I doubt I'll remember your name."

Hurt flashed behind her eyes, making him hate himself a little more, but she didn't back away. "You don't mean that. That isn't what you really feel. What about last night, and the note this morning? You admitted that you care."

"I was trying to let you down easy," he lied. "But clearly you're too stubborn to go along with what's best for you."

"Don't do this." Her bottom lip trembled. "Don't pretend to be awful so you can shut me out. I'm strong enough to make my own decisions and I know what I feel for you is real."

"You think you're in love with a man who hate fucked you for a week, Hannah," he said, his voice hard. "You're either out of your mind or have absolutely no sense of self-worth. Whichever it is, you're in no place to make grand declarations and even if you were, I don't want what you have to offer."

"What's that?" she asked, tears filling her eyes. "Love? Passion? Someone who cares about you for exactly who you are? You don't want any of that?"

"Vanilla sex with a vanilla woman." He let his eyes flick up and down her body, affecting disdain for her simple clothing. “I think you know I have more exotic tastes.”

“So you want to fuck me like you hate me again?” she asked, a challenge in her tone. “Is that it?”

“I don’t want to fuck you at all.”

“Now I know you’re a liar,” she said, reaching for the bottom of her tank top. In seconds, she’d whipped the fabric over her head, baring her gorgeous breasts, which bounced lightly as she unlaced her boots and reached for the close of her shorts.

“Put your shirt on,” he said, struggling to keep his eyes from drifting to her nipples, which were pulling tight in the cool air of the cabin.

He wanted his mouth on her tits and his cock between her legs, but that wasn’t going to happen.

Fucking her again would only make this harder.

“You want me, and I want you,” she shot back, wiggling her shorts over her full hips and pushing both shorts and panties to the floor. “So why don’t you bend me over that desk in the corner?”

She kicked her boots and clothing to the side as she sank to her knees in front of him. “Or maybe you’d rather I take your cock down my throat. All the way in, until I’m choking on you while you fuck my mouth.”

*Shit.* Jackson clenched his jaw, but there

was no fighting the sudden surge of blood to his groin.

She leaned in, her hands coming to rest on his knees as she tilted her head back to look up into his eyes. "And don't you dare tell me you don't want any of that because I can see that you do."

Her hand slid toward his crotch, where his cock had become a hard ridge straining the close of his pants, but he stopped her, his fingers wrapping tightly around her wrist.

"Are you sure you want to play?" he asked. "I don't promise to be nice."

"I don't want to play, sir," she countered. "I want you to fuck me."

"Turn around," he said, grinding the words out, fighting the urge to push her onto her back and take her hard and fast. "Face on the ground, ass in the air."

She held his gaze for a moment before she nodded. "Yes, sir."

She turned to assume the position, giving him an excellent view of the swollen lips of her pussy and the cream filling the well between her legs. She was so fucking beautiful, so strong and obedient, demanding and submissive, all at the same time.

"Reach your hands between your knees," he said as he stood, crossing to the desk where the cloths he'd used to blindfold Hannah on the flight in sat curled in the top drawer. "I'm going to bind your wrists and ankles together.

And then I'll decide whether I want to fuck your ass or your pussy. Do you remember your safe word?"

"Yes, sir." She shivered as he knelt beside her and began to wind the fabric around her ankles and then her wrists. "I've never done that before, sir."

"Are you afraid?" He finished with the last knot and brought his hands to the mounds of her ass, smoothing his palms across her soft skin before using his thumbs to spread her lips wider, revealing the hard pink nub that strained toward him.

"No, sir," she said. "I know you won't hurt me."

"You don't know that," he said, plunging one thumb into her heat before bringing the slick pad to her clit and rubbing in slow circles, drawing a low moan from her throat. "I could rip you in two. I could make sure you limped off this plane bleeding, wishing you'd never met me."

"You could, sir," she said, arching into his attentions. "But you won't."

"You won't speak again until I tell you to." He reached for his belt buckle with his free hand, jerking the leather free and shoving his pants and boxers down around his thighs as he took his cock in hand. He stroked his already engorged length, suddenly desperate to be inside her. "Spread your legs. Wider, Hannah. Show me every inch of what's mine."

She obeyed, spreading her thighs as wide as she could with her ankles tied together, sending a rush of need surging through him so fierce it made his head spin.

By the time the world stopped reeling, his cock was at her entrance and he was shoving into Hannah's pussy, spearing through her swollen walls, feeling her inner muscles clench around him as he sank into her all the way to the hilt.

"I'm going to make you come," he said, bringing his fingers around to tease her clit as he began to thrust in and out. "And when I feel you go, and my cock is slick with your heat, I'm going to take your ass."

Hannah's breath hitched, but she didn't speak. She only squirmed beneath him, welcoming the flicks of his fingers between her legs.

"You aren't to speak until you're given permission, except to say your safe word," he continued, the thought of fucking her in a way no man ever had making his balls ache and his erection swell even thicker. "If I hear your safe word before you come, I'll stop and untie you. If I don't, I'm going to fuck your ass. You'll take every inch of me, even if it hurts."

Her breath rushed out, but she didn't speak. The only response was a gush of heat around his cock that made him ride her harder, fighting the urge to come. She made him want to lose control like no woman ever had.

Which made rising to the challenge of topping her that much more intoxicating.

"You're almost there," he said, fingers flying back and forth across her clit as her inner walls tightened around him. "I want you to tell me when you come. I want you to scream my name and tell me you're coming."

She whimpered, her hips undulating wildly as she sought what she needed to go and he plunged into her again and again, until her pussy was a vice squeezing his cock in two and he knew he could only hold on a few more seconds.

He was about to lose it when she arched beneath him and cried out—

"Jackson, I'm coming!"

With a groan, he pulled out. Smoothing the slickness from her pussy up to her second hole with shaking hands, he got her as wet as he could before giving in to the need screaming through his veins. Fitting his aching cock to her ass he pushed slowly inside until his plump head popped through the tight outer ring into where she was even tighter.

So tight he was afraid he was going to hurt her if he tried to move.

"Breathe, Hannah." He groaned, fingers digging into the flesh of her hips as he forced himself to hold still, giving her body time to adjust. "Breathe and relax."

"It burns, sir," she said, her breath coming faster.

"That's because you're fighting me," he said, teasing her with the shallowest of thrusts as he ran one hand back and forth across the small of her back, urging her to let go of the tension tightening her lower body. "Stop fighting and let me in. Just breathe and let me in."

"I don't know if I can," she whispered, her thighs trembling.

"Then use your safe word," he said as he slid a centimeter deeper. "That's what it's for."

"No, sir," she said, her breath rushing out. "I don't want to give up. I want to take you there. I want all of you."

"Then we'll go slow." He reached down, freeing her wrists from the cloth before guiding her onto her side and lying down behind her. "You should be able to relax in this position. Let go, relax every muscle, one by one."

He ran a hand up and down the side of her body, from her ribs to the curve of her hip and down to her thigh. "Start with your jaw. Let it go, let the tension melt and disappear. Now focus on your neck, feel the places where you're tight and give the muscles permission to stop working."

As he talked his way down her body, urging her to relax, muscle by muscle, he smoothed his palm down her stomach and between her legs, finding her clit and applying the barest pressure.

By the time he reached her middle and lower back, she was relaxed enough to allow him to glide into her another two inches. By the time he reached her thighs and knees, her breath was coming faster and his cock was almost all the way in.

By the time he talked her ankles and arches into a state of softness, she was mewling softly low in her throat and arching her hips, giving him permission to move.

He slid out and back in again, burying his face in the sweet skin at the back of her neck as he fought for control. "God, I love fucking this ass, Hannah. My ass. Only mine."

"Yours," she echoed. "And you're mine and you're not leaving."

"You're not giving the orders right now, sunshine," he said, punctuating his words with a sharper thrust of his hips, making her yip in surprise. "Your only job is to take me inside you and don't come again until I tell you it's time."

"Yes, sir," she said, spreading her thighs slightly, giving his fingers more room to move.

He welcomed the distraction from how insanely good it felt to be driving in and out of her tightness. He played through her slick folds, teasing her aroused flesh, coaxing her back to the breaking point as he gradually picked up speed.

He held on until she was arching into him, her breath coming in frenzied little gasps, and he knew he wouldn't last more than a few seconds.

"Now, baby," he groaned as the dam began to break. "Come for me, sweetness. Now. Now!"

Hannah cried out, coating his hand with fresh wetness as he began to pulse inside her and the world turned upside down the way it always did when he was with her. She fucked the soul from his body, the sense from his head, and left him wanting nothing but more of her. All of her. He wanted to devour her, possess her, and fuck her until she couldn't remember that she'd ever been with any man but him.

Even more frightening, he wanted to stay with her, and forget all the reasons he would never be good enough or gentle enough or man enough for this woman who had given him the greatest gift any person could give: the gift of her entire self, body and soul.

"Sorry," she whispered, pressing his hand to her chest, where her heart thudded heavily against her ribs. "I'm still learning the rules."

"It's all right," he said, his own heart still racing. "But in the future, once we start to play, you follow orders, you don't give them. Save the bossing me around for after I've finished fucking you the way I need to fuck you."

"Okay." She was silent for a moment before she added in a softer voice, "Does that mean you're going to stay?"

He pressed a kiss to the place where her neck became her finely muscled shoulder. She was stronger than her sister in every way, mentally, physically, and emotionally. If there was ever a woman who could survive him, it was Hannah, but he didn't want her to simply survive.

"I want better for you than this. Than me," he confessed, finding it easier to tell the hard truth when she was facing away from him. "I don't know how to love anymore. Maybe I never did. I want you more than I've ever wanted anyone, but I want to possess you, consume you. It's not the same thing."

"I like being possessed and consumed," she said, her fingers playing through the hair on the back of his arm. "If that's all you can give, I'll take it."

"It isn't enough. Eventually, you'll want more."

"Maybe I will, maybe I won't," she said, glancing over her shoulder. "But neither of us will ever know what we want, or how good this could have been if you run away."

He propped up on one arm, staring down into her blue eyes. "How much of yourself are you willing to give up, Hannah? How much are you going to let me take before you draw the line?"

She smiled, seeming sincerely amused by the question. "You don't take anything from me, Jackson. You give me so much. I've never felt more beautiful or powerful or special than I do when I'm with you."

He blinked, surprised though he supposed he shouldn't be. The deeper the game and the more intense the power exchange, the more the lines began to blur. He was the Dominant in their relationship, but only because Hannah was brave enough to abandon control.

Power was a two-way street. The more she gave him, the more he was indebted to her and the more she owned him every bit as much as he owned her.

"But I would like some clothes to keep in my room and permission to call my aunt and check in on her," she continued, granting him respite from his heavy thoughts. "And I'd like to know that I don't have to worry about you running away again. At least for a little while."

He lifted his hand, running his knuckles down her cheek to the tip of her chin. "Ten days."

Her eyebrows lifted. "Ten days until..."

"I'll stay ten days," he said. "At the end of that time I reserve the right to renegotiate."

Her lips quirked, but her eyes remained serious. "All right. Ten days sounds fair. Any thoughts on clothes and phone calls?"

"I have clothes for you," he said. "You can have them when we get back to the house and you can call your aunt whenever you wish. There's a phone in the kitchen and in my bedroom, where you're welcome anytime."

"That sounds nice." Hannah sighed happily. "I like being welcome in your bedroom."

"You're welcome anywhere in the house," he said. "The business portion of our relationship has concluded. From now on, consider yourself my guest."

She wrinkled her nose. "That sounds awfully formal."

"My friend, then," he amended softly. "With benefits."

She smiled. "And rules? Can we make a list of those? I'd like to avoid making any more newbie mistakes if I can manage it."

"No rules outside the bedroom. I'm not a full-time Dominant," he added, smoothing a hand down her thigh. "I like control when we're naked. The rest of the time, you're free to do as you please."

"Free to boss you around?" she teased.

"You can try," he said with a gentle swat on her butt cheek. "But I'm nearly as pig-headed as you are. Expect to have your work cut out for you, sunshine."

"I'm not afraid of hard work," she said, pressing a kiss to his chest that melted something deep inside of him. "But I would like a shower before any more bossing around. The events of this morning have left me feeling adventurous, but also—"

"Like you had a cock up your ass?"

She laughed as a flush crept across her cheeks. "Yes, Jackson. Exactly like that. How did you know?"

"I have a sixth sense when it comes to your body," he said with a wink. "Are you sore? I've got ibuprofen in my suitcase. I can have Adam fetch it before we get back into the car."

She shook her head, her smile fading. "No, I'm not. You were very gentle and patient, the way I knew you would be."

"Smug doesn't look good on you," he lied.

Lying next to him with her skin dewy from making love and her eyes glowing, she was the most beautiful thing he'd ever seen.

And she was his, at least for the next ten days.

He knew he should be ashamed of himself for weakening, but he couldn't seem to feel anything but relief. It wasn't until he had given himself permission to stay that he'd realized how miserable he'd been to leave her.

"Then I'll try to keep the smug to a minimum," she said, brow furrowing. "How about smug on Saturdays until noon and every other Tuesday?"

He leaned down, capturing her lips for a long, slow kiss because she was simply too cute to resist.

"Get dressed," he whispered against her

mouth. “I’ll tell Adam there’s been a change of plans.”

“All right,” she said, then added in a soft voice. “Thank you for staying.”

“Hopefully you’ll still be thanking me in ten days,” he said as he stood, adjusting his pants.

“I hope that too,” she said. “Very much.”

# CHAPTER ELEVEN

## Hannah

Back at the house, Jackson put Adam to work alerting the staff to the change of plans while they retreated to their separate bedrooms to clean up. Hannah was disappointed that Jackson didn't consider joining her in the large shower in her room, but she didn't show it.

He'd come a long way in a single morning, but he was still far from embracing their new relationship with open arms. She wasn't surprised when he elected to keep his distance for a little while and when it was Eva, not Jackson, who brought a small stack of clothes with the tags still attached to her room after she emerged from her shower.

As she spread the dresses and sports clothes out onto the bed, Hannah tried to catch Eva's eye—wondering if she'd spoken to her son and if she too was working for

Hannah's father—but the cook kept her gaze on the floor and retreated as soon as Hannah assured her that she had everything she needed. Dismissing the mystery of Dominic and her family's enemies from her mind for the time being, Hannah slipped into a black and white striped, two-piece bathing suit that made her look like a 1940s pin-up and a semi-sheer black gauze cover-up with embroidery on both sleeves and went in search of breakfast.

It felt strange to leave her room without permission and even stranger to pad barefoot around the empty kitchen, opening drawers and cupboards and otherwise making herself at home. But by the time the oatmeal was simmering on the stovetop and she'd chopped up fruit and almonds for topping, she was beginning to relax. Giving the bubbling pot one last check to make sure the heat wasn't too high, she crossed to the phone on the counter.

A few seconds later, Sybil's voice crackled to life on the other end of the line. "The Mahana Guesthouse. How may I help you?"

"It's me, Syb," Hannah said, her throat tight with emotion. It felt like ages since she'd heard Sybil's voice and so much had happened since she'd said goodbye, none of which she could tell Sybil about. "The phone was installed this morning so I wanted to call and check in."

"Hannah! Sweetheart, it's so good to hear from you." Sybil's smile was practically audible, and Hannah could imagine the way her aunt's kind eyes were crinkling with pleasure. "I know you said you might not be able to call, but I was still worried. Are you enjoying the job? Is the family nice?"

"Yes, I am, and yes, the family is very nice," she said, only feeling the faintest twinge of guilt as the lie slipped from her lips.

She'd told her aunt that she was going to be working as a nanny for a wealthy family while they spent a month decorating their new home on a private island. It had seemed like the kindest choice at the time—if Sybil knew her niece had sold her body to save their home she would be devastated—and it seemed the best choice now. At least until she and Jackson decided that their relationship was going to last for longer than the next ten days.

"So when do I see you?" Sybil asked. "Are you still staying the entire month?"

"Actually, the remodel is going better than expected. I might only be another ten days. I'll let you know when the plans are firm," Hannah said. "So tell me all the news. Have you been able to find anyone to start on the repairs?"

"I have," Sybil said. "Hiro's been an amazing help. We found a father and son team to work on framing the new cottages and I got a bid from the roofers on the other side of the island that's half what our old company quoted. Hiro says they do extraordinary work."

"That's great. I'm glad he's been there to help out," Hannah said, stomach souring at the way her aunt's voice caressed the pearl farmer's name. Before Hannah had learned that Hiro had been Jackson's spy, she'd encouraged her aunt to think about something more than friendship with the man, but now...

"Just be careful, okay," she added. "Hiro seems great, but we really don't know him that well. Sometimes there are ulterior motives with these kinds of deals, and the trusting third party loses out in the end."

"Oh, I doubt it, Hannah," Sybil said before adding in a softer voice. "And I know Hiro much better than I did. We've been seeing each other. Romantically."

Hannah winced as her fears were confirmed. "Really? And it's been...good?"

"It's been wonderful," Sybil gushed. "He's such a gentleman and so kind and thoughtful. You were right. I should have given him a chance a long time ago."

"That's great, Syb," Hannah said, grateful for the hiss of the stove as the oatmeal pot threatened to overflow. "I'm about to burn the kids' breakfast, so I've got to go, but I'll call soon. Take care of yourself, okay?"

"You too, darling," Sybil said. "And call me soon."

Hannah promised to call tomorrow and hung up the phone. She reached the oatmeal pot in time to rescue it from bubbling over and stood scowling at the stove, wishing she'd said something more pointed to her aunt.

She'd promised not to tell Jackson about Dominic, but she hadn't promised to keep secrets from her aunt. Still, there was a chance that Jackson had tapped the phone. It seemed a little paranoid, but he *was* a criminal used to watching his back and a control freak to boot.

*And that's the man you want to live happily ever after with, Hannah. A criminal who you can bet wouldn't like learning that you're keeping secrets from him.*

*Especially a secret like a man in his employ secretly working for someone else.*

"You should have asked Eva to make that for you."

Being careful to keep her thoughts from showing on her face, Hannah looked up to see Jackson standing in the doorway to the kitchen.

# CHAPTER TWELVE

## Hannah

God, he was beautiful, sexier than any man she'd ever met or imagined. In gray suit pants and a white linen shirt that emphasized the bronze of his skin, he looked more like a businessman than a criminal, not to mention good enough to eat.

She smiled, refusing to let stress of any kind ruin their first semi-normal day together. "No, I shouldn't have. I'm perfectly capable of making oatmeal on my own."

"I'm sure you are." He moved to stand on the other side of the island, facing her across the stove. "But I don't want you to have to do anything that makes you frown."

"I wasn't frowning because of the oatmeal," she said as she turned off the burner and pulled the pot away from the heat. "I was just thinking."

"Always a dangerous thing." He held her

gaze, his dark eyes boring a hole through her skin and straight into her soul, making her certain he could read her thoughts. "What were you thinking about?"

"Your job," she said, impulsively. It was at least partly the truth and she didn't like keeping secrets from Jackson if she didn't have to. "I was thinking about how dangerous it must be. It worries me."

"You don't have to worry. I know what I'm doing." He threaded his hands together into a fist as he leaned his forearms on the counter. "But I've decided to take some time away from my work. There's nothing that can't keep until after the holidays and I figure I have enough on my plate at the moment."

Hannah glanced up from the pot, her spoon stilling. "You mean me?"

"I mean you," he confirmed, sending a shiver of awareness across her skin. "I find you take up an inordinate amount of my focus."

She fought a smile. "Well...good."

His eyes narrowed even as his mouth curved. "I thought you were only doing smug on Saturdays and Tuesdays."

"Isn't it Saturday?" she asked, deciding she enjoyed flirting with Jackson almost as much as she enjoyed being naked with the man.

"Thursday."

"Oh, well then. Sorry about that." She lifted one shoulder and let it fall. "Guess my focus has been off, too. I seem to have lost all track of time. Do you want some oatmeal? I have almonds and fruit to put on top."

"Sounds good," he said. "Thank you."

She turned back to the cupboards, chuckling softly to herself as she fetched two bowls.

"What's funny?" he asked when she returned to the stove.

"Nothing," she said, still grinning. "You're just cute when you do normal things like say thank you for your oatmeal."

"I wasn't raised in a barn, either, you know," he said, sliding onto a stool on the other side of the island. "And I'm not cute. Ever."

"I have to disagree, Mr. Hawke." She sprinkled chopped almonds, berries, and pineapple on his oatmeal before placing the bowl and the honey pot in front of him. "There are times when you are adorable."

His smile faded. "And there are times when I'm a nightmare. Don't forget those, Hannah."

"I won't," she said, keeping her tone light. "But it's too early for Broody McScary to come out to play. So be sweet and eat your oatmeal and then we can decide what to do with the rest of the day."

He arched one brow. "You do have a bossy side."

"I know," she said with a wink. "I never claimed to be submissive all the time, either, you know."

He studied her as he reached for his spoon. "I wonder if you're a switch."

"A switch?" She frowned. "What does that mean?"

"A submissive who enjoys taking her turn as the Dominant or vice versa."

She frowned. "I don't know, but I don't think so. I don't like the idea of tying you up." She took a bite, humming beneath her breath as she added more honey to her bowl. "No, I take that back. I do like the idea of tying you up, but not for sexual reasons. Just when you make me angry. There are times when you'd be more manageable tied up."

"And times when I more than earn a spanking?" he asked, eyes sparkling.

"Of course." She licked honey off the tip of her spoon, not missing the way Jackson's eyes followed her tongue. "But that wouldn't be sexual either. In a bedroom situation, I prefer to be the one being spanked."

"And I prefer spanking you," he said, his voice husky.

"So maybe I shouldn't follow the rules all the time," she said, hips swaying back and forth as she leaned her palms onto the counter. "I do enjoy being punished now and then."

"Eat your oatmeal," he said, the intensity in his gaze making her blood rush faster. "Or you'll be eating it cold."

"Why's that?" she asked though she already

knew exactly what was going through his head. There were times when Jackson was a mystery, but there were also times like these when she swore she could read every thought flitting through his beautifully dirty mind.

"Because if I hear one more word out of that pretty mouth, I'm going to have you for breakfast."

Hannah's tongue slipped out to dampen her lips before she whispered, "One word."

Jackson's spoon clattered into his bowl. A moment later he was around the island, pulling her into his arms as he lifted her onto the counter and reached beneath her cover up. As soon as her swimsuit bottom hit the floor, he knelt between her legs, his lips finding where she was already wet and his wicked tongue working its magic. He brought her over twice—once without honey and a second time after drizzling a sticky spoonful across her clit and licking her clean—before he stood and reached for the close of his pants.

"You should put on swim trunks," she panted, hands shaking as she helped push his boxer briefs over the firm mounds of his ass. "Easier access."

"You should stop making me want to fuck you every ten minutes."

Her response died on her lips, becoming a moan of satisfaction as Jackson's cock drove inside her, pushing through her already pulsing flesh. Cupping her buttocks in his big hands, he rode her hard and fast, the urgency in his thrusts making it clear how much it had turned him on to bring her pleasure.

"Yes, Jackson," she said, gasping as he shoved deeper. "God, yes."

"Come for me again," he growled as he claimed her mouth, sending the taste of her own salty heat rushing through her mouth as he kissed her. "Come for me, sunshine."

She obeyed with a ragged cry, her pussy contracting with an intensity that was almost painful. She wasn't sure her body was built to withstand three orgasms in such rapid succession, but she wasn't about to complain, not when she was flooded with such mind-numbing bliss.

Jackson pulled out this time, groaning into her mouth as he pressed his cock between them and came on the fabric of the cover up bunched at her waist. She would have to change again, but who cared?

Not her. She didn't care a bit about cold oatmeal or changing clothes or anything but how perfect it felt to be wrapped in Jackson's arms, catching her breath as they both drifted back to earth.

"Looks like you were right about the timing," he said, kissing her forehead. "I'll have Adam pick up supplies for you when he goes to the market this afternoon."

Hannah's brow furrowed until she glanced down and saw the blood on Jackson's still semi-erect length. "Oh my God," she said, embarrassment rushing through her. "I'm so sorry. I knew it was close to time, but I—"

"Why are you sorry?" he asked, reaching for the dishtowel beside the stove. "There's no reason to be sorry."

"I'm sorry because it's gross," she said, blushing as he cleaned himself and began to wipe away the red smears on her thighs.

"It's not gross. It's part of you and no part of you is gross."

Hannah's lips parted, but before she could think of how to respond to something so sweet, Jackson continued.

"It also means that we've dodged a bullet. If we don't want to use condoms we need to figure out an alternative soon." He knelt down, plucking her swimsuit bottom from the floor and dropping it into her hands. "Maybe an IUD? I can find a doctor to make a house call if you think that's a good option."

She nodded as she eased off the counter, suddenly feeling shy. "That would probably be best. Birth control pills would take too long to work, so...yeah. Let's do that."

He studied her face before asking in a softer voice, "Are you all right?"

"I'm fine," she said, stepping into her suit. "Just a little embarrassed."

"Don't be embarrassed." He squeezed her shoulder gently. "I'm a grown man. I stopped being bothered by things like this a decade ago."

"I believe you," she said with a nervous shrug. "I don't know. I guess it's the birth control talk, too. It makes this seem so much more real."

"I thought that's what you wanted?"

She lifted her gaze. "It is, but that doesn't mean it's not scary." One side of her mouth lifted in a crooked grin. "You're like fire, Jackson. Beautiful, but a little intimidating to get close to."

"I understand." His thumb brushed across her bottom lip. "I feel the same way about you."

"I'm not intimidating," she said with a breathy laugh. Her skin prickled in response to his touch, her body already wanting him again. She felt like she would never get enough of him, not even if their ten days turned into ten thousand.

"No, you're terrifying," he said. "Like a tropical storm, coming to sweep away everything I've worked to build."

"Well, you can always rebuild," she said, strangely flattered by the comparison. "Start fresh from the ground up."

"Maybe I could," he said thoughtfully.

"I called my aunt," Hannah said, sensing that they both needed a change of subject. "She already has a team in place to frame the new cottages."

His hand dropped from her face. “Good. I’m glad she was able to find someone. I know skilled workers can be in short supply on the islands.”

As they washed up and ate their now-cold oatmeal, they continued to chat about safer topics, but Hannah’s mind was never far from Jackson’s words.

Maybe she was his tropical storm. But maybe a tropical storm was what he needed in order to have a shot at turning his life around.

# CHAPTER THIRTEEN

## Jackson

*Six Days Later*

Back when Jackson had been on active duty in the Marines, there never seemed to be enough time.

He was always busy with work and when he wasn't, he was playing as hard as he could, determined to live hard and go to his grave with no regrets.

But since his time in prison, he'd lost awareness of the passage of time. Fueled by rage and obsession, months had faded into years without any change of heart or mind to mark them.

Still if anyone had asked, he would have said his days were full.

But by the start of his seventh day of his new beginning with Hannah, he had realized that before he'd met her, time had been standing still.

With her, hours were devoured in an instant, a day here and gone in the blink of an eye.

It seemed he'd just awoken with her in his arms and already it was dusk and they were wandering along the beach in the sunset light, talking about their plans for tomorrow.

He'd heard that time flew when you were having fun, but it had been so long since he'd experienced anything even close to "fun" that it took a few days for him to recognize the light, pleasantly expectant feeling that filled him when he woke up each morning.

Finally, sometime between picking oranges in the grove with Hannah Saturday afternoon and going for a morning sail around the island Monday morning, it hit him that he was having fun.

Simply sharing a day with her was enough to make it feel like he was on a permanent vacation from the evil in the world, and there was always something to look forward to. There was another moment in her company, another smile, another brush of her lips against his, and the touch of her hand reaching for him between cool sheets.

* * *

By Wednesday morning, he already knew he was going to need more than ten days.

If time kept flying by at this rate, he might need a hundred.

It was a sobering thought, and one that made him keep to himself more than he had since the morning Hannah pulled him off the plane. He ate breakfast alone in his room and worked on answering email and paying bills until nearly ten o'clock.

When he finally emerged, Hannah was nowhere to be found, but there was a note on the kitchen counter saying that she'd gone to the beach and that if he wanted to he should come join her.

Of course he wanted to.

All he wanted was to be with her, but taking too much time off from work could wreck his business. If he was out of the loop for an extended period of time, his connections would find new places to buy and sell their weapons, and he would be out of a job.

He had a good amount of money stored away, but not enough to continue living the way he had for the past several years.

*But you don't have to live that way anymore.*

*Harley's dead.*

*You can let the detectives go, call off the hunt, and start thinking about what you want to do with what's left of your life.*

As Jackson stepped outside and started down the road to the beach, he began to imagine again what it might be like to let go, to let Hurricane Hannah finish destroying the man he had been and see what sort of creature would arise from the ashes.

Maybe it wouldn't be a monster or a man who felt uneasy when a day passed more perfectly than expected.

Maybe it would be someone new, someone who would know how to take proper care of the beautiful woman rocking back and forth in the hammock in front of him, so absorbed in her book she didn't notice him until he leaned against the palm tree near her feet.

"Oh my God," she said, flinching so hard her book tumbled to the ground as she started laughing. "You scared me. I was just getting to the good part."

He knelt, picking up her paperback and shaking the sand off before glancing at the cover. "Another murder mystery?"

"Adam bought it for me yesterday when he was in Moorea." She scooted back on the hammock and drew her legs into her chest. "I don't know why I'm so addicted to them. I usually prefer something with a happy ending and a lower body count."

He returned the novel before easing into the hammock across from her and holding the netted rope out to one side to make room for her legs. Closing the book she stretched out, curling her toes beneath his ribs.

Despite the warmth of the day, he could feel her chilled skin through his tee shirt.

But then, her toes were always cold.

It was one of the many things he'd learned about Hannah since he'd become incapable of thinking about anything else for more than a few minutes at a time.

"Maybe my dark side is rubbing off on you," he said, capturing one of her feet and warming it between his hands.

She smiled. "I don't think so. It's the puzzle aspect that's appealing. I have a few puzzles I'd like to solve." Her smile faded. Her toes wiggled against his palm before she added in a softer voice, "That's why I've decided to tell you my last name."

His hands stilled, but before he could decide whether he wanted the information she was offering, she pushed on—

"It's Mason. My father is Stewart Mason. He won a senate seat in North Carolina a few years ago so you might have heard of him."

"The name's familiar," he said, his throat dry despite the coconut water he'd downed with breakfast. "Your family is wealthy."

"Very," Hannah said bluntly. "My mother's family had more money than God and my father's side made hers look two steps from the poor house." She smiled, but it didn't reach her eyes. "*Fortune 500* magazine covered their wedding. An aerial shot of the estate where I grew up made the cover."

Jackson grunted as he dug his thumb into the arch of her foot, massaging her instep.

There went his theory that Harley had grown up on the wrong side of the tracks and been forced into what she'd done. An heiress wasn't the kind of person who was easily pushed around; she was more the kind to do the pushing.

"That's all you're going to say?" Hannah prodded his ribs with her free toes. "Ugh?"

"So you've decided I'm not crazy?" he asked, lifting his gaze to hers. "Or at least not too crazy to trust with your secret?"

"No, I don't think you're crazy." Hannah cocked her head, shooting him a wry look. "You've been very well behaved the past week."

"Not the entire week," he said, lifting her foot to his mouth and biting her big toe, making her squeal.

"Stop it." She tried to tug her leg away, but he held on tight. "I'm serious, Jackson, that's disgusting. Feet don't belong in your mouth."

"I put all your other parts in my mouth," he said, biting her little toe right where the flesh peaked in the center. "Some much more exotic than your sweet little toes."

She flushed. "I don't walk on the dirty ground with any of those parts."

"Is this a hard limit?" he asked, his mouth

hovering above an as-yet-unbitten toe. "If it is, you should let me know now."

After a moment she shook her head, her breath rushing out with a sigh. "No, it's not. What are you going to do?"

"If it's not a hard limit? I'm going to keep biting your toes."

"Not about that," she said, refusing to let him off the hook. "About the other. What are you going to do now that you know Harley's last name?"

"I don't know," he said honestly. "Now that I know she's really gone..."

He brought Hannah's foot back to rest on his chest and wrapped his hands around her toned calf, simply because it felt good to touch her. "Even if she were alive, I'm not sure I'd know what to do. I won't lie, I would still want to hurt her. But I wouldn't want to hurt you in the process."

Hannah sat up and leaned in to place her hands gently over his. "If she were still alive, I'd make sure she paid for what she did to you myself."

His lips curved. "I believe you would."

"I'm not joking," Hannah insisted. "I'm very fierce when it comes to the people I love."

Jackson held her fathomless gaze and slowly forgot how to breathe.

It wasn't the first time she'd said it, but it was the first time in the past few days. The first time since he'd started to feel incomplete when he wasn't within touching distance of this woman who affected him like no other.

The first time since he'd begun to suspect that maybe his heart wasn't twisted beyond repair.

"I..." He swallowed the words before they could find their way out into the air.

It was too soon.

Once those words were out, there would be no going back and he didn't trust himself to make promises.

Not yet.

"I was wondering if you'd stay a little longer," he said, hoping he'd covered the awkward moment.

Hannah's eyebrows lifted. "But we're not at the end of the ten days."

"I don't need the full ten days to know that I want more," he said, loving the obvious pleasure that bloomed on her face. "Would you stay and spend the holidays with me? I called my associate who owns the island. It's available through January second if you're free to stay."

"Yes," she said, her megawatt grin fading only a watt or two when she added, "though I might need to fly home for Christmas Day to visit Sybil. We've never been apart on Christmas."

"She could come here," he said. "I'm sure

Eva could make something appropriate for a celebration."

"No way. I could make something and Sybil could help. The staff should have the holiday off." Hannah hesitated, doubt creeping into her shining eyes. "But do you really mean it? You'd be okay with her coming here? Meeting you and finding out about...us?"

*Us.*

Even a few days ago he would have told her there was no such thing as "us", but now...

"Assuming we can come to an agreement about how to label the relationship before she arrives, then yes. I'd like to meet her. And I promise to be on my best behavior."

Before he realized she was moving, Hannah's mouth was on his.

He returned the kiss, humming appreciatively as the salt and honey taste of her filled his mouth.

"What was that for?" he asked when they came up for air, both of them breathing faster.

"For you. For this." She settled on top of him, setting the hammock to swaying gently. "For making me happy."

"You make me happy, too." He ran his palms down her spine to cup her ass. "Thank you for telling me about your family. I won't betray your trust."

"I know you won't," she said with a confidence that touched him. "You have your bad points, but you're not a betrayer."

"What bad points?" he asked as he silently wondered if she were right.

He'd been a smuggler for years, but he'd never cheated a contact or double-crossed a connection. He played rough, but he played fair.

Maybe Hannah saw that.

Maybe she saw him more clearly than he gave her credit for—his good points as well as his bad ones.

"You're stubborn as a mule and twice as nasty when your temper's up," she said, finger drifting slowly down his throat. "But you're slow to anger so the temper is bearable. And the stubborn part I'm willing to forgive since I suffer from a similar condition."

He smiled. "Pig-headed-itis."

"Something like that," she said, kissing her way down the trail she'd drawn with her finger. "Your skin tastes so good."

"Not as good as yours." His fingers slipped beneath the band of her swimsuit bottoms, tracing the curve of her ass cheek. "Have you ever had sex in a hammock?"

She laughed, her breath warm on his throat. "No. And I don't think we should try. We'll tip over and kill ourselves."

"No, we won't," he said, tugging her swimsuit lower on her thighs. "I won't let you fall."

"You can't promise things like that," Hannah whispered. "Some things are beyond your control. Like gravity. And my klutzy side."

"You're not a klutz." He slid one finger into her slickness. "You're unspeakably elegant. Help me get these off."

"I think you may be seeing me through rose-colored glasses," she said, but she shifted to one side, allowing him to pull her bottoms down to her ankles and toss them away.

"I see you as you are," he said, opening the Velcro at the front of his trunks, freeing his erection. "Beautiful."

He gripped her thighs, urging her to move, spreading her slickness along his shaft. "Sweet."

He reached between them, parting the lips of her sex. "And sexy as hell."

He drew her down, impaling her on his cock, groaning as her body fought to slow him down.

She was wet, but she wasn't completely ready to take him.

In the past week, they'd discovered a mutual love of this moment, the initial erotic battle as he demanded entrance and her pussy struggled to adapt, and then the sudden bliss as a gush of slickness eased his way and tension became sweet friction.

It was one of the many things he'd learned about Hannah.

And now, he knew her last name.

But he wasn't thinking about that as he

fucked her in the hammock, making her come twice before he shot himself inside her clutching heat.

* * *

He wasn't thinking about family history when they washed the stickiness from their lovemaking away in the ocean and spent the next hour floating in and out on the waves.

And during their lunch on the lanai and walk through the woods after, all he was thinking about was how much he enjoyed her company.

It wasn't until after dinner, when they were settled on the couch reading—a history of Tahiti for him and the murder mystery for her—and Hannah fell asleep in his lap, that he began to think about the Masons.

He sat watching her sleep, wondering how a family who had raised the extraordinary human being drooling on his leg could have also created a monster. He wondered and wondered until the wondering compelled him to pick up his phone and type a quick text to the detective he still had on retainer.

*Harley Mason was the daughter of Stewart Mason.*

*Find out everything you can.*

Later, he would look back on that moment and wonder what would have happened if he'd resisted temptation, if he'd allowed his love for Hannah to be stronger than his morbid obsession with her sister.

But at the moment, he hadn't admitted that what he felt was love or realized how easy it would be to lose the precious thing he'd found.

# CHAPTER FOURTEEN

## Hannah

*Three Weeks Later*

What did a woman buy for her Dominant lover for Christmas?

Jackson had told her that Adam would pick up anything she ordered at a postage box near the airport the same morning he flew to pick up Sybil for their Christmas Eve celebration. But faced with an Internet filled with holiday offerings, she kept coming up empty.

A collar seemed too over the top, a paddle too blatant, and the tiny diamond earrings that spelled "His" too presumptuous.

She *was* his, but he had yet to stake a formal claim. They'd agreed to tell her aunt that he was related to the family she'd worked for and that they'd started dating during his visit to the island and decided to stay on for a few extra weeks of personal time after the rest of the family returned home.

It was a decent story, but one that could create problems down the line.

What if she and Jackson decided to settle down? Wouldn't Sybil wonder, sooner or later, why his sister and her children never came to visit?

Of course, she hadn't mentioned her concerns to Jackson. It would only scare him and he would withdraw into one of his moods, hiding out in his bedroom until noon, wasting half a precious day they could have spent together.

"For a Dominant man, he's very delicate," she mumbled to the laptop, smiling when a grunt sounded from the other side of the bed.

"I'm reading," Jackson said dryly. "I haven't gone deaf."

"You *are* delicate," she said, wrinkling her nose in frustration "And very difficult to buy for. Can't you give me some idea of what you want?"

"I already have what I want." He pulled the laptop off of her thighs, clicking it closed before setting it on the bedside table with his book on top. "All I want for Christmas is you, wearing nothing but a bow tying your hands behind your back. Preferably, you'll be bent over the end of the bed Christmas morning, waiting for me to wake up and redden your pretty ass."

She grinned, pulse spiking as he rolled on top of her. "But I've been so good. You have no reason to spank me."

"I'm sure I can come up with something," he mumbled into her neck as he kneed her legs apart. "Pull down your shirt. I want your nipples in my mouth."

Hannah hesitated for a moment before deciding she didn't want to wait for Christmas Day for her spanking. Sybil would be in the house then and she didn't trust herself not to make sounds that would carry to the guest bedroom.

Besides, she and Jackson hadn't played in several days.

Sex was amazing with him, no matter what, but she still craved the game.

"No," she said, deliberately omitting the honorific. "I don't feel like being kissed there tonight."

He arched a brow. "Who said I was going to kiss you? Maybe I planned to bite, instead."

She shivered, arousal spiking at she imagined what it would feel like to have his teeth on her sensitive tips. "I don't want to be bitten either."

"Then what do you want, sunshine?" He dropped his hips, pressing his erection between her legs so tight she could feel his cock pulse through her thin satin panties and his pajama pants. "Do you want me to remind you why your pleasure belongs to me?"

She nodded slowly, holding his dark gaze as currents of anticipation zipped back and forth between them, charging the air.

"Because it does. Your pleasure and your pain. They both belong to me." His fingers slipped into her hair, the touch gentle until suddenly it wasn't anymore.

She gasped as his hand fisted tightly at her scalp.

Before she could say, "Yes, sir," he was off the bed, dragging her with him.

It didn't hurt—he had too large a handful of her hair for there to be any strands torn from her scalp—but it made her keenly aware of how strong he was, how powerful, and how easily he could bend her will to his, with or without her permission.

But her permission was what made it hot, not scary, when he opened the sliding door, propelled them both across the patio, and tossed her onto the grass in the darkened garden.

She fell onto her hands and knees, but before she could even think about crawling away, he was in front of her, shoving his pajama pants low on his hips, baring his cock. It bobbed free—long, thick, intimidating, and so gorgeous her mouth watered for a taste of him.

She sat back on her heels, anticipating being told to open her mouth and take him down her throat. Instead, he fisted the base of his length in his hand, guiding his pulsing erection down one side of her face and then the other. His skin was burning hot against her cheek and so soft all she wanted to do was kiss him.

She wanted to lick the pre-cum from the tip of his shaft and suckle his plump head into her mouth, but she stayed still, nerves sizzling as she waited to see what he had planned for her.

"Have you ever had a man come on your face, Hannah?"

"No, sir," she said, heat rushing onto her panties at the thought.

"What about your tits? Have you had a man shoot his cum on your tits?" he asked, leaning down far enough to grab the top of her black camisole with his free hand. A second later, he jerked hard on the fabric, tearing it in two.

Hannah swayed on her knees, fear and arousal rocketing through her as her breasts were freed to the night air. Her logical mind knew this was the game, but her primitive mind insisted any man who would rip away her clothes with such violence was dangerous.

The result of the war between the two sides of herself was lust so intense her pussy began to pulse like a second heart, thudding between her thighs.

"Answer me, Hannah," Jackson said. "Don't make me wait."

"Y-yes, sir," she stammered. "You did. That first day. You came on my tits."

"I'm the only one?" He cupped her breast in his hand, his thumb tracing the outer edge of her nipple, close enough to make her ache for contact, but not close enough to trigger sensation.

"Yes, sir," she said, arching into his touch.

He answered her unspoken plea by slapping her breast hard enough to set it bobbing back and forth and to send a sting of pleasure-pain coursing across her skin.

"You don't make demands," he said. "Not even silent ones. You aren't in charge. The only thing you control is your safe word and whether or not you say it. Now turn around and present your ass."

She hurried to obey, swallowing a bleat of surprise when Jackson reached down, tearing her panties in half before she'd made it all the way onto her forearms.

She bit her lip, fighting the urge to press her thighs together. He would know she was seeking relief from the desire making her clit swell and her pussy slick and he wouldn't be pleased.

"If you're obedient, you will be rewarded with release," Jackson said in a low voice as he knelt behind her. "If you are not, I will come and you will spend the rest of the night with your hands tied to the headboard, wishing you could get a finger between your legs, sobbing because you so desperately need to get off. Do you understand?"

"Yes, sir," Hannah said, muscles tightening as his palms settled on her ass, warming the skin.

"Good." He stroked her flesh with a gentleness that sent her fear spiraling higher. A soft start didn't mean anything. She knew that from the last time he'd reddened her ass. "Now I'm going to show you what happens when you forget who you belong to."

Before she could properly brace herself, he'd delivered two sharp swats to the insides of her thighs. The speed and the unexpected location made her flinch in surprise.

Surprise that he could move so quickly, and surprise that being spanked on her thighs was even more arousing than on her ass. He slapped her again in the same places, the stinging sensation seeming to flow directly up her leg to coil around her entrance, making her body burn.

But not with pain, with longing.

By the time Jackson had reddened her thighs and moved on to her ass, Hannah was trembling all over, her pussy so swollen and wet her arousal had begun to run down the inside of her legs. Slowly, as his rhythm grew faster and the blows harder, the need building in her core became the center of her world.

She was no longer Hannah or even a

woman kneeling before a man, she was a hurting, aching, frantic void.

She was a stinging, grieving, exposed nerve so desperate for contact, for relief, that tears ran down her cheeks. By the time Jackson told her to start counting to fifty, her throat was so tight with misery and wanting she could barely force out the words, but she did.

It was almost over.

God, *surely* it was almost over.

She couldn't take much more. She was so near the edge her voice sounded foreign to her ears, a strained, high-pitched yelp that echoed through the garden, scaring all the other night creatures away.

"Keep counting," Jackson demanded as his hand continued to torment her flaming cheeks, his blows coming so fast she could barely keep up.

But she did and finally, when she cried out, "Fifty!" Jackson delivered her promised reward.

He gripped her hips and positioned his cock, telling her to come at the same moment as he drove inside her.

And come, she did.

Her pussy began to contract before he'd rammed home the first time and kept clenching and releasing, clenching and releasing, as he fucked her so hard his hips slammed into her ass, making it feel like the spanking continued. She came until her entire body was in the midst of one long, never-ending orgasm, until her abdominal muscles ached and her lips went numb and her limbs dissolved into boneless appendages too weak to hold her upright.

By the time pleasure was finally finished with her and she came back to her body, Jackson was carrying her into the bedroom and laying her on the bed.

She sniffed hard, reaching up to swipe the tears from her cheeks, but he captured her hand and laid it gently on her stomach.

"Let me," he said, reaching for a tissue from the bedside table. He dabbed her tear-streaked cheeks and upper lip before positioning the tissue beneath her nose and ordering her to, "Blow."

And so she blew, her mind still so deep in the scene she didn't consider disobeying him. It was only after he'd wiped her nose that she flushed with embarrassment.

"I can blow my own nose," she said, her voice thick and rough.

"Not right now you can't," he said, grabbing another tissue. "Right now I'm taking care of you. Blow."

She blew, studying his expression as he continued to clean her face.

He looked so relaxed and happy, the skin around his eyes no longer pinched and his full mouth resting in a lightly curved position.

"If it makes you this happy to blow my nose, you can do it all the time."

His smile widened. "It's you who make me happy." He cupped her face in his hand, staring deep into her eyes. "Do you know how perfect you are?"

She blinked, emotion making her throat tight though she wasn't sure why. "I don't know."

"It's okay to cry," he said softly. "After an intense scene a lot of feelings can come up. And when that happens, you'll need after care from me and kindness from yourself."

"After care?" Her brow furrowed.

"It's when I help you transition out of the scene. No more power exchange, no more game, just me telling you how beautiful and perfect you are and how much I love you."

Her eyes widened and her breath caught in her throat, but he gave no sign that something momentous had been said. He only leaned down to kiss her forehead and whispered, "I'm going to go run you a bath. I'll be back in a few minutes. Just relax."

"Okay," she said, sucking her lips between her teeth until he'd crossed the room and disappeared into the bathroom. Only when he was out of sight did she allow her smile to burst wide open like a firework exploding across the sky.

He loved her. He *loved* her!

She'd felt love in his touch for weeks, seen

it in his eyes when she looked up to find him watching her while she read or gathered pretty shells from the beach, but to hear it...

To hear it was pure magic.

The trembling at the center of her bones was banished by a giddy rush of happiness and gratitude so intense she wanted to run naked through the garden, howling her delight up at the moon. Instead, she rolled over onto her stomach and pressed her face into the mattress to muffle her squeal of celebration.

He loved her! He loved her!

The three words thrummed through her head like some mystical tattoo, filling her with strength. She bounced off the bed, carried across the room by an adrenaline rush so strong it felt like her heart was going to burst through her chest. She danced around the table where Eva laid their breakfast each morning and spun in a circle with her arms held out wide, coming to a stop facing the door.

If she hadn't, she wouldn't have seen that the door was cracked or that someone stood on the other side.

Her hands flew to cover as much of her nakedness as she could—one arm across her breasts and one hand darting down to shield her sex—as she backed away.

She was about to call for Jackson when Adam stepped into the room, holding a phone out in front of him.

"Dominic sent me." He kept his eyes on the floor, making it clear he wasn't interested in her nudity. "You have to leave now. A helicopter landed on the other side of the island. The men sent to kill you will be here within the hour."

"I have to tell Jackson," Hannah said, her adrenaline rush transforming to a frantic, hunted feeling. "He has to come too."

"He's the reason they found you. Look at his messages," Adam said, gesturing for her to take the phone.

Dread flooded through her, transforming her stomach into a hard knot. With a quick glance over her shoulder to make sure that the entrance to the bathroom was still empty, she took the phone. It didn't take long to see what Jackson had done, but she still didn't want to believe.

She didn't want to believe that he'd lied to her or betrayed her trust and she really didn't want to believe he'd done something like this.

But the proof was right there in the two final messages.

The first was a question from someone called Titan beneath a photograph of a woman Hannah never thought she'd see again. It was Harley, older, with her hair bleached blond and sadness tightening her features, but Harley, no doubt in her mind.

She knew her sister was alive even before

she read the message confirming her suspicion—

*I've tracked Harley Mason—now Baudin—to a small village in southern France. I.D. is 100% certain via image and DNA analysis. How do I proceed?*

The last text was a response from Jackson—

*Kill her.*

The phone clattered to the floor and a sound rose in her throat—half cry of shock, half wail of grief—but she stifled it with a fist pressed tightly to her mouth.

"Hannah? Are you all right?" Jackson called over the sound of the bathwater.

"I'm fine," she called back, but she was anything but fine.

Her sister was alive.

*Alive.*

But maybe not for much longer.

Because Jackson had given the order to kill her. To kill a member of her family, her *sister*.

All his talk about loving her and not wanting to hurt her had been a lie. He was a liar and a killer and she'd been a fool to let herself believe anything else.

The realization made her feel like her heart was being ripped out of her chest, but there was no time to grieve the death of the man she'd thought Jackson was, not if she wanted to leave the island alive.

Heart racing, she spun and hurried to the

closet, grabbing the first dress she laid hands on and pulling it over her head as she crossed back to Adam.

"Let's go," she whispered. "He'll be out any second."

Adam nodded and motioned for her to lead the way. "There's a golf cart out front. I've disabled the car and the other carts. He won't be able to follow us except on foot."

Hannah broke into a run in her bare feet, racing silently through the house and out the front door.

Outside, the world brooded in an ominous bluish-yellow light, the sickly moon hanging in the sky coloring everything in shades of ugly. It was a night for death and betrayal, but she was going to escape.

She would get off this island, away from Jackson, and she would find some way to save her sister's life.

Harley might be a monster, but she was *her* monster, and she didn't deserve a death sentence.

"Hold on." Adam slid onto the golf cart seat beside her. Hannah gripped the metal bar on her right, squeezing tight as the wheels churned through the gravel and the cart zoomed away down the road.

The house was nearly out of sight when she heard Jackson roar her name. "Hannah! Hannah!"

Tears filling her eyes, she set her jaw and kept her eyes on the road in front of her.

There was nothing to gain from looking back.

She had nothing else to say to Jackson Hawke.

Not even goodbye.

# CHAPTER FIFTEEN

## Jackson

As soon as he emerged from the bathroom, Jackson knew something was wrong. The sheets were empty and his cell was lying on the floor halfway between the bed and the door.

Stomach clenching, he quickly crossed the room, his pajama pants whispering ominously in the silence.

Whatever this was about, it wasn't good.

He'd deliberately left his phone in his room when he'd come to bed, not wanting to risk Hannah seeing something she shouldn't.

At least not yet.

If the Titan agency's trip to southern France proved fruitful—if Harley truly was alive and in hiding—then he would tell Hannah what the detectives had uncovered. Until then, there was no point in upsetting her. Or in getting her hopes up.

Hannah hated what Harley had done to him, but the woman was her twin. They shared a bond and Hannah still loved her. No matter how many crimes Harley had committed, Hannah would be thrilled to learn she still had a sister.

He knew there might come a time when he would have to choose between his love for Hannah and his hate for Harley. He also knew that, if that time came, the choice had already been made.

Hannah was all that mattered. She was his heart and soul and the reason he'd returned from the dead. Before her, he might as well have been six feet under.

He'd deluded himself into thinking his life had purpose, but a lust for vengeance wasn't purpose, it was a disease that ate away at your soul, leaving you blind. Before Hannah, his existence had been solid darkness. She'd brought him back to the light and reminded him that there were a hundred thousand things in the world more important than revenge.

There was her smile and her kiss and the way she touched him first thing in the morning, with that hint of hesitation, as if he were a beautiful dream she couldn't quite believe was real. There was her laugh and her sweet spirit and the way she gave herself entirely into his keeping. Her trust humbled him, her heart transformed him, and her happiness was the only thing that mattered.

*She* was all that mattered and now she was gone.

He knew it the moment he picked up the phone.

His conversation with the Titan group was pulled up on the screen, including two new texts. One that confirmed Harley Mason was still alive and a second that issued a kill order, an order he sure as hell hadn't given.

"Hannah!" Jackson dropped the phone and ran, his bare feet slapping on the cool wood floor as he hurried through the darkened house, his heart in his throat and the terrible certainty that Hannah was in danger crawling across his skin.

He emerged into the soft humidity in time to hear a golf cart puttering away from the house.

"Hannah! Hannah!" He screamed her name as loud as he could, but there was no answer. By the time he fell silent, the soft rumble of the cart's engine had faded and there was only the wind, shushing through the palm leaves.

Fighting the urge to chase after her in his bare feet, he sprinted to where the car was parked beneath a wide overhang near the entrance to the kitchen, but a glance at the slashed tires was all it took to assure him he wouldn't be getting anywhere in the Cadillac.

Cursing, he cut across the grass to where

the other golf carts were parked in the equipment shed.

He was halfway to the staff cottages when he heard a woman cry out, followed by a rapid stream of Spanish.

Shifting direction, he circled around Eva's bungalow.

On the other side, he saw the cook sitting on the ground in the soft pool of light from the bulb above her door, cradling her son's bloodied head in her lap.

"Mr. Hawke," she said, reaching a hand toward him. "We need a doctor. Please, we have to get Dominic to a doctor."

"I don't need a doctor, Mama." Dominic sat up with a groan, gently pushing his mother's hands away. "Head wounds bleed a lot. It's not as bad as it looks."

He turned to Jackson, body weaving slightly as he pressed one palm to the flowing wound near his hairline. "Adam's not who you think he is, Mr. Hawke. I believe he means to hurt Hannah. We need to put a guard—"

"Hannah's gone, but I think I know where she went. I heard a golf cart leaving the property," Jackson said, hands balling into fists and the need to run after her becoming almost irresistible. "Tell me what happened. Quickly."

"I was coming to check on my mother," Dominic said, swallowing hard. "Adam stopped me before I could knock on the door. He said he knew I'd been hired to keep

Hannah safe, but that I was going to fail. We struggled. I was close to taking him, but he's working with someone. I was hit on the head from behind and didn't come to until a few minutes ago."

At least two men, Jackson mentally catalogued.

At least two men he had to destroy before they hurt Hannah. That was all that mattered. He could grill Dominic on the rest of his story—especially that part about being hired to protect Hannah—at a later date.

"Stay here," Jackson ordered. "Watch the house. If she comes back detain her somewhere safe until I get back."

"Take my gun." Dominic reached down, pulling a small revolver from a holster hidden beneath his jeans. "If Hannah is still alive, she might not be for long. I believe these men were sent to kill her. If you get a clear shot at them, take it."

Jackson's throat threatened to close as he took the gun and quickly checked to make sure it was loaded. "I don't have time *not* to trust you right now, Dominic. But if you've kept something from me and it leads to Hannah being hurt..."

"I want to keep her safe," the shorter man said. "I swear it."

"For your sake, I hope that's the truth." Without another word, Jackson hurried on to the equipment shed only to find the remaining golf cart had been tampered with. Given thirty minutes with a few wiring tools, he knew he could correct the problem, but he didn't have thirty minutes and neither did Hannah.

Abandoning the shed, he ran back toward the main house. Underneath the lanai, where the beach chairs and umbrellas were stored, sat two lightly rusted bikes. Shoving the gun in the back of his pants, he grabbed the larger of the two, swung onto the seat, and began pumping hard down the road leading away from the estate.

Years of pushing his body to the breaking point had given him thigh muscles of pure steel. He could bike around this entire island twice before he gave out. He would be able to catch up with the cart, and when he did, he wouldn't hesitate to shoot first and ask questions later.

The men in front of him had given up their right to mercy when they'd laid hands on the woman he loved.

He loved her.

He loved her so much, but he'd only said the words once.

He wanted to say them a hundred more times, a thousand. He needed Hannah safe in his arms more than he needed his next breath and by the time he reached the fork in the road and turned instinctively toward the airfield, his heart was threatening to punch a hole through his ribs.

He'd tested the edge of his endurance nearly every day of his adult life, but terror had never been a part of his daily runs or workouts. After he'd been released from prison, he'd assumed he was immune to this kind of fear—a man without a soul doesn't have much to be afraid of—but that was before Hannah. Before her love and before she'd given him something priceless to lose.

He swore beneath his breath, jaw clenching as he pumped even harder.

He told himself the rumble he heard wasn't a plane engine purring to life. Then he told himself that he would reach the field in time to stop the plane from taking off. But he knew he was grasping at straws, knew it even before he saw an unfamiliar aircraft lift into the sky, flying low over his head as he leapt from the bike near the airfield's entrance.

Jackson's head snapped back, but it was too dark to see much of the plane aside from the breadth of the wings and the red stripe running from the nose down toward the belly, illuminated in the spill of the headlights. He didn't know who owned the plane, but he would bet his fortune that Adam was flying the aircraft, which meant his own plane was useless.

He couldn't fly a plane or follow the men who had taken Hannah. He couldn't do anything but stand and watch the aircraft move farther away from the island, heading north before veering slightly to the east and gradually disappearing from sight.

When the sky was empty once more, he did a sweep of the small, shuttered outbuildings and the field, finding two golf carts parked by the gate in the glow of the lamp lighting the area, but there was no sign of Hannah. There was no sign of a struggle either, simply the imprints of her bare feet in the dust next to Adam's larger ones.

There was another set of prints, too, slightly smaller than Adam's that tapered at the toe and had no pattern on the bottom of the shoe. A dress shoe, he guessed, which told him nothing.

He had no idea who Adam was working with, why his most trusted employee had betrayed him, or what he planned to do with Hannah. He only knew that he had never felt more helpless than he did right now, not even on the day he was led away to a cell and locked away for a crime he hadn't committed.

"I'm going to find you," he said softly, staring up at the star-flecked sky in the direction where the plane had flown away. "I'll find you and if they've hurt you, they will pay for it. I swear it."

The vow helped calm the impotent rage burning in his gut.

If there was one thing he was good at, it

was tracking down people who didn't want to be found. He would find Adam, and the man would pay the price for betrayal.

He would pay in pain, suffering ten times the torment for every mark he left on Hannah's skin.

## CHAPTER SIXTEEN

### Hannah

Someone else was flying the plane, but Hannah didn't know who it was. She supposed in some part of her mind, she had assumed it was Dominic. Adam had said that Dominic sent him, after all, and Dominic was the first one to approach her about the dangerous people who might be coming to the island.

But when the aircraft reached cruising altitude and Adam slipped into the cockpit to take over the controls, it wasn't Dom's dark head that ducked through the door leading into the cabin. It was an enormous, silver-haired man with broad shoulders, a strong jaw, and the most familiar pair of brown eyes in his lightly tanned face.

They were Jackson's eyes, but so much colder. Colder even than the day he'd pulled off her blindfold and glared down at her with a ferocity that had made his contempt for her abundantly clear.

Hate was a terrifying thing to see in another person's eyes, but at least it meant that the person still had the capacity to feel deeply. Love and hate were opposite sides of the same coin and shared far more similarities than differences. They both came from the heart and the heart could be reasoned with, appealed to, even changed from time to time. The heart knew how to forgive, and as long as forgiveness was a possibility, hope was never beyond reach.

But this man's eyes were...empty. The windows to his soul had been blown out and any mercy he might once have possessed had escaped into the ether, never to be seen again.

One look at him and Hannah's gut sensed the approach of an enemy. It was all she could do not to cringe in her chair as the terrifying man began to speak.

"Hello, Miss Mason. I'm Ian Hawke. I've come to take you to your sister."

A sudden surge of delight streaked through her fear, but it was gone in an instant, excitement at the thought of seeing Harley too fragile to survive the terror swelling inside her.

Jackson had betrayed her trust in the worst way, but not everything out of his mouth had been a lie. She believed his stories about his father, the cruel man who had never given his son the love a child deserved and had abandoned Jackson without bothering to find out if the charges against his son were true or false. No matter what Ian Hawke said next, she knew the fact that Jackson's father was here wasn't a good thing.

"Why?" she asked. "Why are you taking me to Harley? What do you want?"

The older man smiled, but it was nothing like Jackson's smile. There was no light or joy in it. He was simply baring his teeth, the smile an implied threat that made her pulse speed faster. "You're clever, but not as clever as your sister. We had to drug her to get her onto the plane. She knew better than to trust anyone but herself."

Adrenaline dumped into Hannah's bloodstream, her most primitive instincts screaming for her to run, but there was nowhere to run to. She was trapped in a plane above the ocean with a man who made Jackson look like a teddy bear in comparison, and there would be no escape.

"As for what I want," Ian continued, settling onto the small leather couch next to her seat. "I want your father to pay his debt. If he does, you will be allowed to live."

The tension fisting in her middle eased a bit. If Ian wanted money, her father certainly had enough of it, and he wouldn't hesitate to pay her ransom. For all his faults, Stewart Mason valued her life as much as he valued his fortune. She was about to tell Ian as much when he spoke again.

"I think he'll choose you, anyway," he said, smiling that terrible smile. "You're the good girl, aren't you? The one who always did as she was told? I understand your sister was his favorite once, but when he realizes he can only keep one daughter, I suspect he'll see the wisdom in sparing your life instead of hers."

Only keep one daughter. Only one.

He was taking her to her sister, but she might only have hours with Harley before one of them was murdered.

Acid surged up Hannah's throat. A moment later she was bent double, retching on the floor of the private jet whisking her away to meet the fate she'd been running from for six long years.

To be continued...

Jackson and Hannah's story concludes in
DIVINE DOMINATION
Available Now.

## SNEAK PEEK

*Please enjoy this sneak peek of Divine Domination*
Available Now.

**WARNING: This is a white-hot, panty-melting, boundary-pushing read. Not intended for the faint of heart.**

"You're mine. You belong to me. You will always belong to me. Because no one has ever made you feel the way I have."

Jackson Hawke might be a monster, but he's Hannah's monster. They belong together and she's determined to show Jackson she can love every part of him-light and dark, cruel and gentle, lost soul and Dominant man.

Jackson knows he doesn't deserve her. He

is broken and twisted and wrong inside, but when Hannah touches him it feels right, he feels right in a way he hasn't in so long.

**Can a monster learn to become a man again? Or will dark forces from the past claim Hannah's life before she can claim his heart?**

Jackson had killed before—in combat and once when negotiations with a Mexican drug cartel had gone awry and he'd had no choice but to kill or be killed—but he had never experienced anything like the blood lust pulsing through his veins as he steered the abandoned golf cart he'd found at the airstrip back toward the villa.

When he got his hands on the men who had kidnapped Hannah, he was going to rip their hearts, still beating, from their chests and stuff the organs down their throats. He was going to pull them limb from limb and toss the pieces of their mutilated bodies into the sea. Or maybe he'd leave them out for buzzards to pick at and maggots to writhe inside.

Every fate he imagined for the men was more horrible than the last, but no amount of terror, pain, or desecration seemed sufficient punishment for the sin of taking Hannah away from him.

And if Dominic were correct, and the men intended to kill her...

Jackson swallowed hard, forcing down the gorge rising in his throat.

They would beg for death by the time he was through with them. They would *beg* for it. Jackson had no doubt he could deliver enough suffering to make Hannah's kidnappers sorry they'd ever heard her name, but that wouldn't bring her back. Once she was gone, she would be gone forever—and his heart and soul along with her.

He had to get to her before it was too late for both of them.

He parked the cart by the lanai and took the steps up to the villa two at a time. He found Eva and Dominic in the kitchen talking animatedly in Spanish, but their conversation cut off abruptly when he entered the room.

"I was too late." Jackson aimed himself at the phone, where Hannah had called her aunt nearly every day for the past month, trying not to think about the way her sweet laughter had filled the room as she chatted with the woman who was like a mother to her.

He would hear that laughter again. But first he would hear the screams of the men who had taken her away from him.

"They left on a small private plane," he continued. "The jet is still here, but I can't fly it. I'll have to hire a charter and see how fast they can—"

"We can take my jet," Dominic said. "I've already put in a call to the pilot in Moorea. He should be landing soon. And I've got a tech team hacking into a surveillance satellite orbiting the area. Hopefully, they'll be able to get a visual and tell us where the plane is headed."

Jackson slammed the phone back into the receiver before turning to shoot Dom his most threatening look. "Who are you? Who are you working for and why should I trust you when you knew Hannah was in danger and failed to protect her?"

"I'm working for her father, Stewart Mason," Dom said, as his mother angled her body in front of his, clearly intending to protect her son from Jackson, even if her employer was twice her size. "I've been working for Mr. Mason for years, trying to keep Hannah safe from those who mean her harm."

Dominic paused, eyes narrowing as he shook his head back and forth. "And then you showed up. At first, I thought you were part of it. But you really have no idea, do you?"

"No idea about what?" Jackson growled.

"About your father," Dom hurried on, clearly sensing Jackson's mounting frustration. "He's the one who killed Hannah's cousins. He's trying to take out all of Stewart Mason's heirs."

Jackson's brows drew together so sharply it

sent a flash of pain through his temples. "My father is a real estate developer. He's a cold hearted bastard, but he doesn't kill people." He frowned harder. "And even if he did, why would he give a shit about Mason's money or his heirs? My father is a wealthy man. The last thing he needs is more money."

"Story too long," Eva piped up, waving a hand at Jackson before turning back to her son. "Is too long and Hannah in trouble. You work together. Help her. Then you fight."

The seemingly sincere concern in the older woman's voice reminded Jackson of his other source of information, the one person he trusted wanted nothing but the best for Hannah. "I'm calling her aunt." He snatched the phone up with one hand as he pointed at Dom with the other. "Get my cell from the floor in Hannah's room. As soon as I'm finished with this call, I have to place another one. Then we'll talk."

He should probably call the Titan group first. He doubted Alexander Titan would initiate an execution based on a text message —especially since they'd never discussed the price for murder on demand—but Hannah was his first concern.

He would do what he could to keep Harley safe, but only after he found out who had Hannah and was on his way to getting her back.

Sybil answered on the third ring, saying,

"Hello, darling, is everything all right?" in a sleepy voice.

A glance at the clock above the stove revealed it was nearly midnight. Jackson had been so terrified he hadn't even noticed the time.

"No, Sybil, it's not. This is Jackson, Hannah's friend," he said, wincing at the last word. He was so much more than her friend, but her aunt had never met him or seen him and Hannah together. She might not trust him enough to open up about their family secrets, but he had to try, for Hannah's sake. "I'm sorry to be the one to tell you this, but something terrible has happened. Hannah's been taken. By two men, one of whom I thought I could trust with my life."

"Oh my God," Sybil whispered.

"I realized she was missing and followed them, but it was too late," he continued, knowing he didn't have time to waste explaining all the finer—and crazier—details of Hannah's abduction. "I got to the airfield in time to see their plane take off. My plane is still here, but I don't have a pilot so I couldn't follow them."

"Hannah's been taken," Sybil said, speaking to someone on the other end of the line. "And her friend can't fly the plane. Do you think—"

"There's a man here who claims he works for Hannah's father," Jackson broke in. "He says there's a plane on the way that we can use to go after her, but I don't know if I can trust him."

"Well, you don't really have a choice, do you?" Sybil's voice was surprisingly strong and steady. "You have to get to her as soon as possible, Jackson. If they took her alive, she won't be alive for long. I've already lost three brothers and four nieces and nephews to this nightmare. I can't lose Hannah, too. She's like a daughter to me."

Jackson leaned against the kitchen counter, fear prickling across his skin. Could Dominic be right about his father?

"The man here said that someone is killing the Mason heirs," he said, deliberately keeping things vague to see if Sybil would confirm Dom's claim. "Do you know why? It might help me figure out where they've taken Hannah."

"It has something to do with my brother, Stewart," Sybil said after only a moment's hesitation, evidently deciding to trust him. "Over the years, he's received threats from an old business partner. But when I've pushed for more information about the threats or the partner, he refuses to speak about it or to go to the authorities for help. He has deliberately kept the assassinations of our family members a secret while concealing the other man's identity and I... Well, I believe I know why."

"Why?" Jackson pressed, his thoughts racing.

Was his father the old business partner? It was easy to imagine Ian bending the law to crush a rival, but murder wasn't part of the tax code. As far as Jackson knew, his father had never even had a parking ticket. He was a decorated Marine, a self-made man who had married into one of the oldest families on the eastern seaboard. He wasn't a mob boss for God's sake.

*You were a decorated Marine, and look how far you've fallen. Maybe you inherited more from dear old dad than height and the color of your eyes.*

"I think Stewart had something to do with what happened to our brothers," Sybil said in a pained voice. "He's always been different and they bullied him terribly when he was small. I was the only one who was kind to Stewart and I am the only one who didn't meet with an unfortunate accident in the fall of 1975, just weeks before our father's will was set to be read."

She sighed, the sound making it clear how heavily her suspicions had weighed on her. "I've had too much time to think to believe that's a coincidence. I was spared because Stewart told the person he'd hired to kill the others to let me live. But then, I assume something must have happened to make the killer turn on him." She paused before continuing in a haunted tone, "And now Stewart has spent the past forty years defending his family from a nightmare that he set in motion, knowing his connection to the murderer would be obvious if anyone ever learned the man's name."

"You could be right," Jackson said, his throat tight. "I'm going to look into a few things, Sybil. I'll call you back."

"I'll come to you," Sybil said. "My friend Hiro is a pilot. He says he can borrow a plane and get us both there in ninety minutes. When you figure out where they've taken Hannah, we'll come with you."

*Her friend, Hiro.* Jackson was tempted to tell the woman her trust was grossly misplaced but resisted the urge.

Hiro had been his spy, but he'd also said he cared about Sybil and sounded like he meant it. If there was one thing Jackson had learned from his time on the island, it was that people could change. Even the hardest heart could soften in the hands of the right person. Hannah had transformed him, given him back his soul and a reason for living. If Sybil had done the same for Hiro, Jackson wouldn't do anything to ruin the happiness they'd found.

But he would do what it took to keep Sybil safe. It's what Hannah would want.

"No," he said. "Pack what you need for a week or two and have Hiro fly you somewhere no one will think to look for you. You can give me his cell number and I'll call you as soon as I have any updates on the situation."

"But I—"

"I know you want to help find Hannah," Jackson interrupted gently. "But the people who have taken her are dangerous. Hannah loves you more than anything. If I brought you into a situation that would put your life in danger, she would have my balls for breakfast."

Sybil's laugh ended in a soft sob. "Sounds like you know her well. Most people think she's a pushover. They don't see how strong she really is."

"I see her," Jackson said roughly. "And I love her and I swear to you I will get her back or die trying."

"Don't die," Sybil said. "There's been enough death and Hannah needs you. She loves you very much, too, Jackson. And I'm sure she knows you're doing everything you can to reach her."

"I hope so," he said, falling silent as Sybil gave him Hiro's familiar number and he pretended to write it down.

He hoped that Hannah believed he loved her. Or that he'd at least have the chance to explain that he hadn't given the kill order she must have seen on his phone.

He didn't care enough about Harley to want to kill her. Not anymore. His hate had faded to a two-dimensional emotion, one that could be folded and put away in a box inside of him and left to quietly decompose. The only passion he felt now was for Hannah, for her safety, her love, and the chance to build a life with the woman who had made him believe in miracles.

She was his miracle, his savior, his heart, and he was going to find her. He couldn't be too late. He couldn't have come so far out of the darkness only to lose his light.

Divine Domination is
Available Now.

# ACKNOWLEDGMENTS

First and foremost, thank you to my readers.

Every email has meant so much. I can't express how deeply grateful I am for the chance to entertain you.

More big thanks to my Street Team, who I am convinced are the sweetest, funniest, kindest group of people around. You inspire me and keep me going. I'm not sure I'd be one third as productive without you.

Big tackle hugs to all.

More thanks to Kara H. for organizational excellence and helping me get the word out. (No one would have heard of the books without you!)

Thanks to the Facebook groups who have welcomed me, to the bloggers who have taken a chance on the books, and to everyone who has taken time out of their day to write and post a review. I appreciate you!

## TELL EVERLY YOUR FAVORITE PART!

I love reading your thoughts about the books and your review matters. Reviews help readers find new-to-them authors to enjoy. So if you could take a moment to leave a review letting me know your favorite part of the story—nothing fancy required, even a sentence or two would be wonderful—I would be deeply grateful.

## ABOUT THE AUTHOR

EVERLY STONE writes dark, dangerous, action-packed romance. Love Dominant Alpha males and strong women who know what they want—in bed and out of it?

Start with the Bought by the Billionaire series!

Learn more at Everly's site https://www.everlystone.com.

Everly also writes sexy contemporary romance and laugh out loud romantic comedy as Lili Valente. Learn more at www.lilivalente.com

## ALSO BY EVERLY STONE

Learn more at Everly's website

https://www.everlystone.com.

* * *

**Bought by the Billionaire**

**The Series**

(HOT novellas, must be read in order)

*Dark Domination*

*Deep Domination*

*Desperate Domination*

*Divine Domination*

**Kidnapped by the Billionaire**

**The Series**

(HOT novellas, must be read in order)

*Filthy Wicked Love*

*Crazy Beautiful Love*

*One More Shameless Night*

**Under His Command**

**The Series**

(HOT novellas, must be read in order)

*Controlling her Pleasure*

*Commanding her Trust*

*Claiming her Heart*

**The Snowed in Series**

*Snowbound with the Billionaire*

*Snowed in with the Boss*

www.ingramcontent.com/pod-product-compliance
Lightning Source LLC
Chambersburg PA
CBHW061250120726
48001CB00001B/248

*9798739775160*